# Street Soldier 2

## Silhouettes

URBAN
BOOKS

*www.urbanbooks.net*

Urban Books, LLC
78 East Industry Court
Deer Park, NY 11729

ISBN 13: 978-1-60162-508-3
ISBN 10: 1-60162-508-1

First Printing June 2012
Printed in the United States of America

10 9 8 7 6 5 4 3 2 1

*This is a work of fiction. Any references or similarities to actual events, real people, living, or dead, or to real locales are intended to give the novel a sense of reality. Any similarity in other names, characters, places, and incidents is entirely coincidental.*

Distributed by Kensington Publishing Corp.
Submit Wholesale Orders to:
Kensington Publishing Corp.
C/O Penguin Group (USA) Inc.
Attention: Order Processing
405 Murray Hill Parkway
East Rutherford, NJ 07073-2316
Phone: 1-800-526-0275
Fax: 1-800-227-9604

# Street Soldier 2

## Silhouettes

# Chapter One

## When Love Calls, Ignore It . . .

Say what you want, but didn't too many people give a fuck about black-on-black crime in St. Louis, the city known for being in the top-ten most dangerous. If they did, I wouldn't have never been able to wipe out the three niggas who killed my baby's mama, Nadine, and get away with such a heinous crime. Yeah, the police had been lurking around, asking questions, but after three months or, possibly, the first forty-eight hours, I assumed Nadine's case was put in a file and never looked at again.

That's why I, Jamal Prince Perkins, had to get back to business around here. At first, I was skeptical about killing the fools who took Nadine's life, but with my son being in the car that was riddled with bullets that day, I figured those niggas didn't give a fuck about me, so in no way did I care about what I'd done to them. The only setback that happened was Nadine's mom was so distraught about how shit had went down, a month later she jetted with my son. I went to go pick him up one day and the whole house was empty. I knew she had held me responsible for what had happened to Nadine and, to this day, I felt the same. Mama tried to convince me that everything happened for a reason, but I could in no way see the logic behind Nadine being killed instead of me. She had just graduated from high school and was looking forward to going to a community college. No doubt, she had a bright future ahead of her and my son had a pretty decent mother.

As for me . . . I was just an okay father, but had made some changes in my life so I could be there for my son like I needed to be. Having him at eighteen was tough, but I had to quickly give up my "boy" status and become a man. Proving that I was a real Street Soldier was imperative, and that meant getting a job to provide for my son; a son who I didn't know if or when I would ever see again. That shit hurt me like hell, but it wouldn't be the first time I had to deal with setbacks in my life. This was the norm, and like always, I had to brush that shit off and keep it moving.

I wasn't working for On-time Delivery Services anymore. I was doing things on my own. I ran a laundromat business that was going strong, as well as a liquor store that was right across the street from it on Union Boulevard. Hired an old black man, Nate, who I could trust with running the liquor store, because the niggas I had known from the hood wasn't about nothing. They were all out to see what they could get, and the only one I had ever trusted was my boy, Romeo. He was still locked down in prison, and with a thirty-year bid for an accessory to murder conviction, it would be a long time before we would ever see each other again. I never visited him, because he didn't want me to. I couldn't stand to see him behind bars. We wrote letters to each other and I made sure he didn't want for nothing. At twenty years old, I was still reaping the benefits from the money I received after killing my deadbeat-ass father. I had sense enough to make it stretch so I could do what I needed to do. In no way would I say I was balling, but I did have enough money to live comfortably and get by. Stealing, robbing folks, and hustling were no longer in my game plan and, for that, I felt as if I was on the come up. Hopefully, my shaky past was behind me and no retaliation for the murders I committed was ordered.

Hell couldn't be as hot as the laundromat was, and, as I sat in a chair sending Mama a text message about the items she wanted me to bring her, I could see what looked to be sweat dripping from the antique white walls. Two round floor fans sat in each corner, but they weren't doing nothing but blowing out more hot air. The smell of overly hot dryers, as well as Bounce fabric softener, infused the air. The whole damn place was stuffy, but all I was concerned about was making money.

About ten ladies were inside doing their laundry. A few kids were running around, and some were behaving while looking at the flat-screen TV I had mounted on a wall. I tuned out the noise. After I sent Mama a text confirming what to bring, I got up to get a soda from a soda machine. My lips were dry and my flowing, neatly cut waves were shining from the sheen on my hair. I wiped my forehead, then swiped my hands on my heavy-starched denim jeans that hung low. After getting my soda, I couldn't wait to pop the top and get back to my seat. The cold soda going down my throat felt good, and as I watched a woman enter with seven clear trash bags filled with clothes, I could only smile to myself, feeling I was in the right business.

"It would be nice if I could get some damn help with this," she yelled out to a heavyset man who slowly trailed behind her. He seemed occupied with his phone call and the last thing on his mind was helping the woman with her clothes. She snatched up two of the laundry carts, and started to pack them high with the dirty clothes she had in trash bags. Since I was sitting nearby, I could smell the stench from the clothes. It was obvious that the woman hadn't washed in quite some time. Looked like she hadn't washed her ass, either, and the perspiration spots underneath her armpits and the dirt piled underneath her fingernails suggested that she hadn't seen something as simple as water. As she fussed about doing everything all by herself, the man who was with her paid her no mind. He leaned against one of the folding tables, still indulging in his conversation.

Spending so much of my time in the laundromat, I felt the bullshit about to go down. I got up from my seat, but was stopped by a woman who complained to me about the change machine being broke.

"I put five dollars in there and only got back four quarters. The same thing happened to me the last time I was here. That machine be gyppin' people out of they money."

She was so loud and close to my ear that I backed away, not wanting her to get close to the two-carat diamond in my earlobe, or bust my eardrum. I was almost 110 percent sure that the woman had put a dollar in the machine, but I was in no mood to argue with my customers. Instead, I reached into my pocket and gave the woman four dollars worth of quarters. She walked away and, just for the hell of it, I put a dollar and a five dollar bill in the machine. To no surprise, it gave me the correct change. I cut my eyes at the woman who was trying to be slick and made my way toward my tiny office in the back. Before I got there, I listened to the irate woman and her man go at it. Everyone was pretty much tuned in, even the kids who had stopped running around to listen.

"You are lazy, Tim, and I don't give a shit who knows it! You need to get off that phone and wash your own damn dirty drawers!"

"And you need to shut the fuck up and keep your fat ass movin'. My drawers ain't the only ones dirty and look at yo' stained panties."

"At least I'm willing to wash mine," she fired back. "You . . ." she said, picking up a pair of his drawers, swinging them in the air. It looked like the brotha had skidded in some mud and I, along with everyone else in the laundromat, was frowning. Some of the kids were holding their noses, as if they could smell his drawers. "You expect for me to wash these? Please! Put that damn phone down and wash your own shit!"

The man shifted his eyes around the laundromat, looking embarrassed as hell. He didn't have much else to say and, as the woman separated his clothes from hers, he stood with his arms folded. She kept cussing and fussing. As soon as I turned, that's when I heard a loud thud.

"Daaaaamn," one woman shouted. "He didn't just hit her, did he?"

I saw another woman nod, and I watched as the man stood over the woman who had dropped to the floor, pointing at her. "I told you about that shit, didn't I? All you do is run your fat fuckin' mouth. I get tired of hearin' it! Wash these damn clothes and call a cab when you're done! I'm out of here."

Everyone was in awe, including me. Now, I had witnessed shit like this all the time, thanks to Mama and her men. My gut always told me to stay the fuck out of it, because nine times out of ten, the woman was going to stick with her man. From a short distance, I could hear the woman wailing out loudly, and I eyeballed another one of my customers who walked up to the man. She looked to be about five feet five, and weighed less than 150 pounds. Most of her hair was shaved off and was perfectly lined. She had some of the smoothest brown skin I had ever seen, and diva was written all over her. Her breasts were tiny as hell, but I could see the size of her nipples through the white spaghetti-strap tank she wore. The faded jeans she rocked had rips in them, but they plumped her ass up to stand at attention. She was no match for the 300-pound man who stood before her, but her bravery was admirable. She pointed her finger close to his face and her chipped long nail nearly touched his nose.

"That shit was uncalled for," she said with a twisted look on her face. Her hazel-green pretty eyes, like Rihanna's, showed no fear and were lethal. "Your fat ass should know better, and if you hit her again while in my presence, I'ma do something about it."

The man smirked and cocked his head back. "Bitch, get out my face. This between me and my woman, and you ain't got nothin' to do with it."

"I got your bitch," she said, reaching out her hand to help the woman off the floor. Obviously, she had a bunch of mouth but was afraid to get off the floor and challenge the man who had dropped her. Without saying a word, she wiped her tears, shooting daggers at the man with an embarrassing and devious look. The man threw his hand back at both women and headed toward the door, mumbling underneath his breath. I couldn't hear what he'd said, but the brave chick did. She made her way up to him, holding out her hands.

"A baldhead bitch I may be, but I bet you won't put your hands on me like you just did her. Try me, motherfucka. Stop talking that mess and try me."

The man's eyes twitched and I saw him tighten his fists. He looked like a grizzly bear and I suspected he was about to knock the woman on her ass, so I decided to intervene. Just in the nick of time, I stood between them, touching the man's heaving chest. I could tell that the chick's aggressiveness had him fired up, but she wasn't backing down. I turned to him first.

"Man, you gon' have to go. I can't have you up in here fightin' with my customers. Don't force me to call the police on you, dig?"

The man stood for a moment, but didn't say another word. He soon pushed the door open and made his way outside. The chick who approached him rolled her eyes, then yelled out, "Sloppy, fat-ass punk!"

She walked up to the other woman who kept thanking her for intervening.

"You really didn't have to involve yourself like that, but I appreciate it. Sorry about that, though. I'm truly sorry."

"No worries," the mad chick said. "But you don't need to be involved with a man who treats you like that. I don't know you at all, but that was not a good look."

The woman dropped her head in shame and two more ladies walked over to offer their opinions and support. They started to help the woman with her clothes, and as soon as I walked by, I heard one of them say, "Niggas ain't shit."

"None of them," the brave one added. "He was in here and didn't say shit! What kind of man just stand there and watch a lady get knocked the fuck out by a man? He could have said something, but since he up in here looking like Trey Songz, I guess he think he looks too good to get involved."

I halted my steps and pointed at my chest. "Are you talkin' to me, Miss Rihanna wannabe, or are you talkin' about me?"

"If the shoe fits, wear it," she responded while rolling her neck.

I was in no mood to argue with this bitch, who, for some reason, had a chip on her shoulder. I also hated a smart-mouth chick, and if I gave her the attention she wanted, the police would definitely have to show their faces. "Whatever. Hurry the fuck up with your laundry and get your mean ass out of here before I put you out."

"I'd like to see that happen. And, as soon as my clothes get done drying, you don't ever have to worry about me coming back here again. I won't, and I will make sure that my other friends and family members don't either. You don't deserve my business and, since you can't even put a man in his place for wronging a woman, maybe you can spend your money on a damn air conditioner to cool off your customers."

"Maybe you can take the advice of the man who left and shut the fuck up. Like he said, it wasn't your business, and the woman you're rushin' to protect will be somewhere tonight with his dick in her mouth or ass. You're wastin' your time. Your business: don't need it. You can get your wet clothes out of my dryer right now, and take that shit fourteen blocks to the next location. No loss here."

The other women stood with their mouths hanging open. I was in no mood to argue with any of them. I didn't want to lose their business either, and as they continued to rant I walked away. I started sweeping the floor then noticed that Miss Meany must have taken my advice, because she stormed over to the dryer to get her clothes. She slammed them into one of the laundry carts, steadily talking about how much "niggas ain't shit." It was apparent that she had some deep shit going on inside, and the frustration showed on her face. I had even noticed her smack away a tear, and I couldn't believe it was that serious.

Feeling a slight bit bad about losing her business, and about what I had said to her, I walked up to her. She was putting her wet towels in another basket.

"Go ahead and finish dryin' your clothes," I said. "I apologize for what I said to you. I do appreciate yo' business."

She ignored me and continued to remove her towels. I found her stubbornness to be sort of sexy, but not the mean mug on her face. The straps of her tank kept falling down and she pouted while putting her straps back on her shoulders.

"Did you hear what I said?" I asked.

No answer. Her towels were all in the laundry cart and her clothes were in another one. She rolled the carts toward the door, but one of the kids ran into it. One cart fell over, knocking her wet clothes on the floor.

"Dang, watch where y'all going," she shouted at one of the kids who knocked her cart over. The kid didn't even apologize, just laughed as the chick bent down to pick up her stuff. The mother walked over to apologize, but she was ignored as well. I had already tried to calm her down, but it was obvious that she wanted to be left alone. She rushed outside, filled the trunk of her red Ford Focus, and left. I shrugged and headed back to my office. It was barely big enough for a desk and two chairs inside, and was also where I kept some of my laundry detergent to fill the machines. Some items were in a closet. Needing a quick nap, I laid my head on the desk and closed my eyes. Within seconds, I was out.

It had to be less than thirty minutes later when I was awakened by a knock on the door. I wiped the dripping saliva from the corner of my mouth and rubbed my tired eyes.

"What's up?" I asked the person on the other side of the door.

"I need change," a woman said. "The change machine is out of coins."

I opened the door and gave the woman change for three dollars. When I checked the coin machine, it was indeed out of coins, so I had to fill it. Just as I was doing so, I felt a tap on my shoulder. "Somebody lost this," a youngster said, handing me a purple wallet.

I thanked him, then finished filling the coin machine, stocked the detergent machine as well, and swept the floor again. Afterward, I went back to my office, and almost forgetting about the wallet, I pulled it out of my pocket. When I opened it, there was a driver's license inside that belonged to the mean chick from earlier today. Her name was Poetry Wright and she lived nearby on Page Boulevard. I snickered as I saw her name, and went through her wallet to see what else I could find. She had a few pictures inside, about forty-two dollars, a food stamp card, and a pair of tiny diamond earrings that were wrapped in plastic. I didn't know if the earrings were real, but I opened my drawer and dropped the wallet inside. I thought about trying to find her number, or possibly going to her house to take her the wallet, but as shitty as she was to me, I squashed the thought. I got up to go clean the nasty-ass bathroom that was next to my office, and had to find a plunger for the overflowing toilet piled high with shit. I gagged, trying to clean up the mess, and once I was finished, I sprayed the bathroom down with Lysol. I took the trash to the dumpster behind the laundromat, and as soon as I got back inside, I saw Poetry coming through the front door. She walked to where she had been, moving newspaper out of the way and looking underneath the tables. I was leaned against one of the tables in the far back, pretending to be interested with the cartoons on the TV.

"Excuse me," she said, heading my way. "Have you seen a wallet in here?"

I ignored her, until she got close to me. "Wha . . . what did you say? I didn't hear you."

"Have you seen a purple wallet?"

"Maybe," I said, keeping my eyes on the TV.

She waved her hand in front of my face. "It's either yes or no. Have you?"

Her attitude was working the shit out of me. "No, I haven't seen nothin'."

"Well, why did you say maybe then?"

"Because I felt like sayin' it, that's why."

She rolled her eyes at me and continued with her search. After nearly fifteen minutes of looking around, she headed for the door. I wanted to fuck with her, so I yelled out her name.

"Poetry!"

Her head snapped to the side and she turned around. "How do you know my name?"

I shrugged and walked toward her. "I just guessed it. Besides, you look like you could be a poet, and I bet that when you put all of that madness aside, there's a real sweet side to you."

She held out her hand, displaying no smile on her face. "Give me my wallet."

I slapped my hand against hers and shook it. "Poetry, Prince Perkins. If you want your wallet, you gon' have to get at me better than that."

She pulled her hand back and folded her arms. "Prince? What kind of name is that? You damn sure ain't charming. Can I please have my wallet?"

"We won't even go there with the names, but at least you know ain't shit charmin' about me. You're so right," I said, winking at her. "But, I can be nice when I want to be. Follow me."

Poetry followed as I made my way to my office. She stood in the doorway, watching me remove her wallet from my drawer. I handed it to her.

"Here you go. Some young man found it and gave it to me. I don't know if he took anything out of it, but at least he didn't take your driver's license."

She opened her wallet and looked through it. "Yeah, my license is in here, but I had a fifty dollar bill in here, too. Either he took it, or you did."

I defensively held out my hands. "I didn't take nothin'. Fifty dollars ain't enough for me to steal, but I wish the young man was still here so you could confront him instead of me."

"I wish he was too, but I have a feeling about where my money went."

She turned around and I was pretty uptight that she, in her own way, had called me a thief. Not only that, but she didn't even thank me for giving the wallet to her. I rushed out of my office, hurrying behind her.

"Thank you too, you ungrateful ass . . ."

She turned around, halting the word that was about to slip from my mouth. "Thank you for what?" she said. "For stealing my money? Okay . . . thanks, Prince Perkins, for stealing my money. I had an electric bill to pay, but thanks to you, this bitch's electric will be getting cut off."

She hurried outside, and only because I was getting accused of something that I didn't do, I chased behind her, fuming. "Listen, you dumbass-actin' chick. I didn't take your money. But since you think niggas ain't shit, here," I said, reaching into my pocket. I had a wad of dollar bills that covered several hundreds. I pulled a hundred away from my wad and reached out to drop the bill down her top. "Take that shit and pay your damn electric bill. Make sure you get the money, before it slip through those tiny-ass titties of yours. Be gone, and for the record, yo' ass ain't welcome back to my laundromat again. Peace!"

I walked off and she started laughing. I didn't see what the fuck was so funny, but maybe she knew, so I asked.

"You are. Getting all uptight and shit. I was only kidding with you about the fifty dollars, but you damn sure won't get this hundred back. Thanks, Prince. For my wallet and for my mani and pedicure you just paid for. I'll be sure to come back and show them to you."

This chick was seriously about to get hurt. This is why I didn't fuck with nobody on a regular basis and it was also why I had so little respect for women. They played too many damn games, were liars, and didn't know how to keep their big mouths shut. I decided not to waste any more of my time or energy on this chick. This was a wrap, and all I could say was she'd better hope like hell that I never saw her again.

# Chapter Two

## Same Ol', Same Ol',
## Some Things Never Change

Things had settled down at the laundromat, so I stopped by the liquor store to see how things were going with Nate. He said business was booming, and I could tell it was by how many people were standing in line. Nate stood behind the tall glass windows that separated him from the customers on the other side. A cigar dangled from his mouth and he scratched his bald head as he waited for a customer to count out pennies for a can of Stag beer. The customers behind him were frustrated and so was Nate.

"Say, man," Nate said to the wrinkled-face man. "Why don't you move over to the side and count out your money? I need to tackle this line real quick, all right?"

The man nodded his head, and moved over so Nate could wait on the other customers. I'd seen the man in the store before, and nearly everyone knew that he was a neighborhood crackhead. His beady eyes shifted around, and realizing that he was short on money, he asked one of the customers in line for twenty-five cents.

"Nigga, back up," the man shouted. "I can't stand no beggin' motherfuckas!"

Nate just shook his head, and so did I. And unable to pay for his beer, the man walked out the door.

"His ass always comin' in here short on change,"
Nate griped. "I guess he think I'ma give him that shit
for free, but that ain't happenin'."

"It better not be," I said, smiling as I sat on a stool
behind him. I wasn't in business to give nobody nothing for free. If people were willing to pay the white man
for his products, then they damn sure had to pay me.
The only person who got shit free from me was Mama.
I had to look out for her, even though she hadn't been
looking out for herself. She was still seeing Raylo's
abusive ass. We had squashed our beef with each other
some time ago, but I still didn't like the fact that he was
hitting on my mama. For years, he'd been saying that
shit would stop, but it hadn't. I guess they had this kind
of relationship where that kind of head-banging mess
was okay. If she was cool with it, I had to be. But I knew
that it would be near impossible for me to continue
living with her under those conditions. Eventually,
somebody would get hurt and I didn't want it to be me.
That's why I moved out and never looked back. Mama
and Raylo could continue their dysfunctional life, as I
wanted no part of it.

Before I left the liquor store, I helped Nate knock out
a few customers, then I filled a brown paper bag with
the items Mama had asked for earlier, which were a
bottle of ketchup, some mayo, a Vess Soda, and some
Doritos. She also needed some aspirin for her headache, and when I got to her house on Goodfellow Boulevard, I definitely knew why. The whole left side of her
face was fucked up and I didn't have to ask why.

"Don't be looking at me like that," she said, taking
the brown paper bag from my hand. "I asked for this
stuff four hours ago, Prince. Had my mouth set for
some potato salad and I don't even want it now."

Yeah, she wanted it, but I ignored her tone. It's the way she and I got down, and even though we loved each other, the respect wasn't quite there. Not as far as conversation was concerned, but I was doing my best to change some things around. I was getting older and was starting to realize some things that I hadn't seen before. Mama may have had some serious issues, but when it came down to it, she was there for me when I needed her to be—sometimes.

"You're welcome," I said, taking the bag away from her. I placed it on the kitchen table and pulled the mayo out from inside. "Here. Better late than never. Go ahead and fix the potato salad. I haven't eaten all day and I'm hungry."

She snatched the mayo from my hand and started to whip up the potato salad. I put the other items on the counter, then headed back to the cramped bedroom that used to be mine. Mama still had everything left as I'd had it, and had even taken it upon herself to keep it clean. I wasn't the tidiest person in the world, and my one-bedroom studio apartment above the laundromat was a mess. Maybe I could talk Mama into stopping by and cleaning up for me. She often griped when she stopped by to see me, but it never failed that she would call me trifling or nasty before she left. I told her to call before coming over, but Mama wasn't one to play by my rules. She showed up whenever she felt like it, and many times my place looked as if a tornado had run through it.

Thing was, I could never get down with cleaning like she could, and I didn't have a woman—well, no one on a regular basis—who could do it for me, either. For now, I was sticking and moving with my neighbor who was fifteen years older than I was, and with a chick named Francine who had moved into the same building about a month ago. It was hard trying to juggle the two of them, but they both knew it was just a fuck thing for me. Since Nadine had been killed, and since I'd found out that the woman schoolteacher I'd been fucking was my sister, Patrice, I chilled with the whole relationship thing. I wasn't feeling that shit at all, and at this point, it was all about making money: money for me, for my son I was dying to see again, or for the one who I still had no ties to. Word on the street was I'd had another son by a chick named Monesha that I swapped juices with in high school. She gave me a STD, so that caused me to leave her ass behind. I was never really sure if the baby was mine, but the truth had always weighed heavily on my mind. There was one way to clear it up, and that was by making one simple phone call. Thing was, I just wasn't there yet. My life was on a peaceful path, and I wasn't ready for Monesha's whack ass to be a part of it again.

I sat on my twin bed that was neatly made, looking at the mail Mama always left for me. There was a cable bill that I agreed to pay for, and my cell phone bill was there, too. Some junk mail was included, and even a card from Romeo that was sent to my mother on her birthday. Why she put it on my bed, I wasn't sure. I tucked the pieces of mail in my pocket and made my way back into the kitchen. Mama was scooping some potato salad on a plate that already had several slices of saucy, meaty ribs on it. Raylo was the one who knew how to barbecue his ass off, so I suspected he had cooked the meat.

"The 'cue smells good," I said, sitting at the table. Mama put the plate in front of me, and kindly poured me a cup of the strawberry Vess Soda. She fixed her plate then sat at the table with me. I couldn't help but be discouraged by the bruise on her face.

"What did y'all fight about this time?" I asked.

Mama bit into one of the ribs before responding, "None of your damn business. And, how do you know Raylo did this to me?"

"Who else did it, Mama? A ghost? I wasn't born yesterday, and we both know that shit has been goin' on for years."

"If that's the case, then don't sit your tail over there actin' all brand new. If you think my face is bad, you should see his." She laughed. "I fucked his tail up, then made him cook me some barbecue."

Finding no humor in Mama's comment, I shrugged and changed the subject. "Why you leave Romeo's card on my bed? He sent that to you for your birthday, didn't he?"

"Yes, but I don't accept mail from jailbirds. Romeo fucked up his life, and I'm just glad that you ain't get yourself caught up in no mess like that. I know what you did after Nadine was killed, but that shit was justified. Just hope you're done with that kind of foolishness. I've been proud of you for handling your business. Real proud."

I wanted to fall out of my chair. Mama's words had left me speechless. I had never heard her say that she was proud of me, and to hear her say it today just did something to me. A chill ran over my body and I kept staring at her as she lowered her head to eat. Over the last year or so, our relationship had changed. When I had Prince Jr., she seemed to come back to life. We had spent more time together and a lot of the money that I had I used to help her get on her feet. She was always a beautiful woman to me, but had let herself go down over the years. I remember my friends always comparing her to Diana Ross, and that made me feel proud. The abuse that she had taken from the men in her life, especially Raylo, had taken its toll. And to still be going through that shit at almost forty years old, it didn't make sense to me. That's why I hated when Nadine's mother took Prince Jr. away. Mama's life seemed to go flat again, and even though she hadn't said much about him, I knew she was missing his presence as I was.

"You haven't heard anything from Nadine's mom, have you?" I asked.

Mama picked at her food, still looking down. "Why would I hear anything from her? That bitch was wrong for what she did, and if I ever see her again, I'm going to tell her about herself. I doubt that she'll call me, and what you need to do is go to the police and tell them she kidnapped your damn child. Make them arrest that heifer. She had no right to do what she did and I miss my baby around here."

I felt what Mama was saying, but I wasn't one to run to the police for anything. They'd start asking questions about me, and I didn't want them putting two and two together about what I had done. Mama seemed to be getting upset, so I hurried to change the subject.

"I'll tell Romeo how you feel about him sending things to you, that way he doesn't waste his time. And, as for you being proud of me, thanks. I needed to hear that."

Finally, Mama looked up and smiled. We got down on our food, and when Raylo came in, he had to find something to fuss about.

"Fool, why you got that Camaro parked in my driveway? I had to park on the street. When a man comes home, he likes to park in his own driveway. As soon as you get time, move yo' car so I can get my car off the street, before one of those niggas out there hit it."

Mama pursed her lips and rolled her eyes. She had been standing up to Raylo a lot, even though it caused her some damage. "Prince only comes here about once or twice a week. Ain't nobody gon' mess with that raggedy-ass Cadillac of yours. You can wait until he leaves, can't you?"

"No, I can't," Raylo said, looking at me. "Either move yo' car, or I'll move it for you."

How he intended to do that without any keys puzzled the hell out of me. And don't get me wrong, Raylo was a big and strong old dude who definitely had some muscles. But, moving a car? Not. Not mine anyway, but to prevent any arguments from transpiring, I got up from the kitchen table to go move my car.

"Thank you," Raylo said in a sarcastic tone. He and I were just okay, but lately he'd been seeming kind of jealous of me. He used to make money by slanging dope, but for some reason much of that had been put on hold. I was doing my shit the legit way, and to be honest, I thought it kind of bothered him a bit. Why? Didn't know, but I chalked it up as another nigga hating.

I moved my Camaro, parking it on the street. I knew I wasn't going to be staying much longer, and as I heard Mama and Raylo arguing all the way outside, I hurried inside. I could barely get a word in over the loud screaming and yelling, but was finally able to say, "I'm out," to my mama.

"Take some of this food with you," she said, but Raylo had something to say about that.

"He makes enough money to buy his own food. Let him fend for himself. We barely have shit over here to eat! I didn't stand outside for hours and hours for somebody to come over here and eat up my damn food!"

Mama shot a dirty look at Raylo, then she piled more ribs on my plate, wrapping it in aluminum foil. "Here," she said, shoving the plate toward me. "And if you want some more, you're welcome to it. I paid for that meat with my own money and ain't no damn nigga gon' tell me not to feed my own son."

"Bitch, you ain't worked since 1982. What money did you use to pay for that meat? I paid for it, and if I don't want Prince to have none of it, he won't get it!"

I was starting to get a headache. They went back and forth about who paid for what and what I could or should not have. "Fuck it!" I yelled. "Ain't no big deal, Mama, 'cause I already ate. Y'all get on my nerves with this shit and that's why I hate comin' over here. Don't y'all ever get tired of arguin'? Damn!"

They both turned to me, looking as if I were the one out of line. Mama pointed her finger at me. "Keep your mouth shut, Prince. Now, take this damn food and get on out of here."

Raylo didn't say nothing else. He stormed off toward the bedroom, slamming the door behind him.

I took the plate from Mama's hand. "Thanks," I said, kissing her cheek, because I was still on high from her telling me she was proud of me. "I'll stop by in a few days. Let me know if you need anything."

Mama nodded, and as we walked to the door, I could not help but ask her, "Why do you keep puttin' up with his shit? It's timeout, ain't it?"

Mama threw her hand back. "Just let it be, Prince. You know I got this. I always have, haven't I?"

Not to me she didn't, but I left it at that. I seriously wondered if or when enough would be enough. Or, when it would be too late for Mama to get herself out of such a fucked-up situation.

I returned to the laundromat, only to find it crowded as ever. Somebody had a radio on that was blasting so loudly I could hear it outside. If I didn't know any better, I would have sworn that I was at a nightclub or something. Ladies were standing around yakking and the kids running around were driving me crazy. I couldn't do nothing but smile at one of the ladies who was sitting down, minding her own business and reading a book.

"Whose radio is this?" I asked with my hand already touching the cord to unplug it from the outlet.

"Mine," one lady said. "Is there a problem?"

I snatched the plug from the outlet. "Yeah, there's a problem. My electric bill is already too high."

The lady pursed her lips, but didn't give me any gripe. I could hear some of the others whispering under their breath. Good or bad comments, I didn't care. I kept it moving to my office, but stopped as I smelled something horrible coming from the bathroom. When I opened the door, vomit was all over the floor. The stench made my stomach turn, and I swear I wanted to throw these women and their kids out of my establishment. I was sure somebody knew who the hell had thrown up, but was too damn lazy to clean it up. I went to the closet to get a mop and bucket. But as soon as I strolled the bucket of water with Pine-Sol in it into the bathroom, my neighbor and fuck partner, Francine, came up from behind.

"I thought I'd find you here," she said, looking down at the vomit. She could see the irritated look on my face, and without saying one word, she took the mop from my hand. "Go sit down. I got this. I've been looking for you for a while, but didn't see you."

"I went to the liquor store, then stopped at my mama's house. Why were you lookin' for me?"

Francine rolled the mop around on the floor while frowning. She was a bit on the chubby side, but was cute as hell. Had a round face with curly hair that was kind of molded into an afro. I had a thing for Jill Scott, and Francine definitely took me there. Plus, she had a motherly thing about her that I loved. Simply put, she was nice. Kind of took care of me, and looked out for me all the time. When she'd cook something, she always brought me a taste of whatever she cooked. She gave me good advice, but one thing we had in common was being messy. Her studio apartment wasn't what I would call spotless, but it was decent. We clicked better with each other because she was only twenty-two, two years older than me. The fact that she was a stone-cold freak made me appreciate her even more.

"I wanted to tell you that Mr. Jefferson came by looking for his rent money. Did you forget he was coming?" she asked.

I stood in the doorway, and patted my back pocket for the money order I'd gotten earlier for my rent. "No, I didn't forget. He just be showin' up and expectin' people to always be home when he get here. I'll drop it in his mailbox when I go back upstairs."

"Well, I told him I would remind you. I know you have a lot on your plate, and you sometimes forget about things. Just like you forgot about taking me to the grocery store last week. I caught the bus, but it wasn't no fun lugging all those groceries back from Aldi."

"I already apologized for that. Had some business to tend to. You should have reminded me."

"Business like what? Screwing Jenay's old ass? I saw her creeping out of your apartment, but you know I'm not gon' trip, right?"

"I should plead the fifth, only because you don't want me to comment about nobody creepin' in and out of your apartment, do you?"

Francine smiled, knowing that she kept niggas running in and out of her apartment. She had a high sex drive and was the first to admit it. Her being with other men in no way bothered me, and if anything, what we had was all about getting sexual pleasure. She could suck the skin off my dick, and as good as her head job was, she was free to do it any time.

"No, don't comment," she said, laughing. "I catch your drift, but you still played me though."

"Not intentionally."

"Maybe not, but I was still left . . ."

Francine continued to talk, but I didn't pay her much attention because from the doorway I could see Miss Poetry getting out of her Ford Focus. I figured she was back to cause trouble. She headed my way, but I turned my head in another direction.

"I know you see me, *boy*," she said. "Why you turn your head?"

I pulled my cell phone from my pocket, pretending as if I would use it to call the police. Surely, though, this chick I could handle. "What do you want? Why you keep buggin' me, ma?" I asked.

"What I want, you can't give me. That would be a decent man, who stands up and protects a woman when need be."

"Protect women? Maybe. Hoodrats? No. Sorry, and if it applies, don't be mad at me."

Francine had stepped outside of the bathroom to see who I was talking to. She glanced at Poetry, who seemed angry, but still looked sexy as hell. Poetry put her hand on her hip while staring at Francine.

"Can I help you with something?" Poetry asked.

"Nope," Francine said, handing the mop over to me. "I'm going back to my apartment. Have fun and see you later." She wiggled her fingers at me, waving good-bye, but cut her eyes at Poetry.

For the hell of it, I playfully smacked Francine on her meaty ass, causing all of it to jiggle. She couldn't help but blush. "Prince, you need to quit, *boy*. Bye."

I winked and let out a sigh as my attention turned back to Miss Attitude who kept running her mouth. "I assume you were referring to the woman from earlier as a hoodrat, so I'ma let what you said slide," she said. "The real reason why I came back was to show you what your money paid for and to thank you for being so kind."

She held out her hands, just so I could see her perfectly polished nails. Then she had the nerve to look down and wiggle her toes that were visible by the thong sandals she wore. The polish was a lime green with designs on it.

"Now, that's some ugly shit," I said, walking away from her and into my office.

"Ugly," she shouted, following me. "How can you say my nails look ugly? You probably don't know nothing about polish anyway so forget you."

"I know enough to say that shit on your fingers and toes look awful. I thought you were ghetto before, but now I'm much more convinced."

She couldn't wait to start rolling her neck, even though I was just playing with her. "Ghetto? You think I'm ghetto? Negro, please. You're the one ghetto, and look at how you dressed. Jeans all sagging. Shirt too damn big. Name all jacked up, and who in the hell go around answering to Prince? The only Prince I know is from the 1970s or 80s. He sang 'Purple Rain,' and unlike him, you do not have it like that to be calling yourself no Prince."

"Oh, I got it like that, bet. A Prince I am, and Prince I will always be." I removed my white oversized T-shirt that covered the carved muscles on my chest. STREET

SOLDIER was still tattooed down my chest and my mother's name, Shante, was scripted on there as well. With my jeans hanging low, Poetry got a good look at my body that I always kept in shape and cut to perfection. Her eyes were glued to me, but her lips were pursed.

"I guess your mouth is twisted because you need to contain those liquids formin' in your mouth," I said. "And a shirt or pants don't make a *man* ghetto, the way he conducts himself does. Just like the way you do. By your actions, I have to assume that you are Princess Ghetto and it appears that you wear your crown well."

Poetry dropped her hand from her hip, but folded her arms across her chest instead. The rolling of her neck ceased. "That's fair, but ghetto or not, you like it."

I cocked my head back. "Tuh. What makes you think that?"

"'Cause I know these kinds of things. But since you prefer to play hard to get, I'ma leave you with this." She reached into her pocket. "Here's your hundred dollars back. Like I said, I was just fuckin' wit' you, and I don't need your money. And I got something else for you, too."

I took the hundred from her, waiting to see what else she had. She went back into her purse and reached for a pen on my desk to write something. She reached out to give the piece of paper to me. I took it.

"That's my phone number," she said. "If you're interested, use it. If not, your loss."

Poetry turned to walk away, and I couldn't help myself from taking a look at her nice ass that fit well into her torn jeans that showed some skin peeking through the holes.

"Poetry," I said, this time walking behind her. She turned and I happily tore up her number and dropped it in the trash can beside me. I swiped my hands to-

gether. "Thanks, but no thanks. You got too much attitude for me, and *girls* like you don't move me."

She snapped her fingers. "Damn. If chubby ones did,
I was so sure I would too. But like I said, your loss, *boy*,
not mine."

She walked out, leaving me to wonder if I had made
a big mistake by tossing out her number. I revisited all
that had happened today, pretty positive that I'd done
the right thing. To me, she was trouble. Trouble that I
didn't need.

# Chapter Three

## The Past Is Never Behind Me . . .

I was lying on my sofa sleeper with the windows wide open. No breeze was stirring and the blue sheer curtains were at standstill. Sweat ran from my forehead and since the air conditioner was broke, I regretted giving Mr. Jefferson my rent money. He hadn't come by to fix the air since I'd reported it broken three days ago. This was the kind of shit that frustrated me the most, and when it came to me spending my money, I expected things to be taken care of. The only complaint that I didn't have right now was with Francine. As I sat with gripes about what wasn't going right, there was no doubt that I was pleased with her skillfully sucking my dick. She had it gripped with her hands, taking it all in like a pro. My eyes were fluttering and I couldn't tell if the sweat was from being so hot from the stuffy room, or from what she was doing to me. I felt like I was in a coma. Didn't dare to move and my mouth was sealed tight.

"I know, Prince," she said, taking a few seconds to break. "You like . . . love this, don't you?"

All I did was nod. Francine inched me to the verge of busting a nut, and when she felt my dick pulsating, she backed away from it. She straddled my lap, and lifted her ruffled skirt above her hips. I had all hips and ass in my hands, trying to maneuver my hard muscle into her wetness as she squatted. She slammed down on me several times, causing my body to jerk from her aggressiveness.

"Damn, ma. Take it easy. What's the rush?" I asked.

"No rush," she said. "I just like fucking you, that's all."

With that, I kept my mouth shut, and let Francine do her thing. By the time we were done, which was about an hour later, the smell of sweaty sex filled my entire studio apartment and I had blown through three condoms. I'm not saying it wasn't worth it, but as Francine lay sprawled out on my sofa sleeper, asleep, it was time for her to go. I wanted to go check on Nate at the liquor store and there was no way I was leaving anyone in my apartment without me being there. I shook her shoulder, causing her to roll over on her back and yawn.

"What time is it?" she asked, stretching her arms.

"Almost seven in the P.M. I need to go check on the store, so I'ma need you to jet. We can hook up later, all right?"

Francine tossed the covers aside and quickly got dressed. We both headed down the hardwood-covered hallway that led to an elevator. As soon as it opened, Jenay stepped off, smiling and speaking to both me and Francine. I spoke, but Francine didn't.

"Be good, Prince," was all Jenay said and kept it moving. The upside to her was that she didn't give a fuck about nothing. She minded her own business and was cordial to everyone in the building. Yeah, she knew what time it was with me and Francine, but she wasn't the kind of woman to trip off no twenty-year-old and who I was fucking. I liked that shit about her, and her maturity played a big part in us having a connection that suited both of us. We only fucked when she wanted to, and that was more rare than one would think, only because Jenay was bisexual. She loved women more than she did men, but still required some dick from time to time. I was definitely down with that, and since she'd let me in on a few of her threesomes before, I wasn't one to complain.

I crossed over Union Boulevard, making my way to the other side of the street. Like clockwork, Nate was behind the counter waiting on several customers. The only time he took a break was for lunch. Either I would come to the store to relieve him, or he would close the store for an hour. His one-bedroom apartment was above the liquor store and that was to both of our benefits. I had someone I could depend on, and I paid him well for being just as committed to my business as I was.

"Sup," he said, tossing his head back as I opened the door to go behind the counter with him. I slammed my hand against his, laughing at the way he was dressed. For him, wearing blue jean bibs, Stacy Adams, and a baseball cap was the style. He was too old school for me but I guessed at fifty-nine years old he felt his attire was appropriate.

"You know you be killin' me," I said, sitting on the stool behind him. Nate knew exactly what I was talking about, because I had shot him down several times about the clothes he wore.

"What did I tell you," he said. "You don't know nothin' about the way a for-real man is supposed to dress, and the only thing you got goin' on is that diamond in your ear. You around here with those saggin'-ass clothes on, tryin' to look hip, but lookin' like a slouch. I ain't never seen you in one thing I would have worn back in my day, and when I tell you this Negro right here had it goin' on, I mean it."

I laughed as Nate got back to waiting on the customers. This time, a woman was short ninety-two cents for her items and he looked over at me. "She short. I normally don't let nobody slide, but . . ."

"I don't care if she's short a penny. I need to get paid, man, and unless you want me to take it out of your salary, go ahead and make the call."

He looked at the woman who stood with an attitude. Nate was like me—he didn't like women with attitude or those looking for freebees. Obviously, she fucked herself without knowing it. "Sorry, babes. You gon' have to put somethin' back. We expect full payment in here."

"Not always," she challenged. "You let my friend get some stuff on credit last week. But you gon' trip with me over ninety-something cents? Just cancel my stuff. I'll go elsewhere."

"I don't have a problem with that, Miss Lady. And just so you know, ain't nobody came in here and gotten shit on credit. Y'all need to learn how to pay up or stay the hell out of here. Now move out of the way so I can wait on other payin' customers."

The woman stormed off after snatching her change from the revolving window. "People always want somethin' for nothin'. Do you know how many times that kind of shit go down in here? I don't know why they think I'ma give them somethin' for free."

I laid the word find puzzle book on the counter and bent down to circle the word I'd found. "Maybe because you've been in here givin' people stuff away on credit. That's what she said, ain't it?"

"I know you don't believe that shit, do you?"

"Hell, nah. That's just to get you to give her somethin'. I like how you handled that, and male or female . . . if they ain't got the money, they don't get the product."

Nate slammed his hand against mine and continued to wait on customers. I worked my puzzle then got up to use the bathroom. No sooner than I returned, I heard some fools outside of the liquor store arguing. I looked through the window to take a peek. Nate didn't seem alarmed by the ongoing threats that were coming from outside, and when he eyeballed the twelve-gauge shotgun that was leaned against the counter for protection, I knew he had us covered.

"What can I get you, sir?" he asked the older gentleman who didn't respond because he was listening to the ongoing ruckus outside. And, before we all knew it, several people rushed inside to prevent themselves from being hit by the stray bullets that were piercing the air outside.

"Get down on the floor," one man shouted while shielding a woman next to him.

"Damn!" a lady said while yelling for her kids to get on the floor. Nate had the shotgun in his hand and I dropped to the floor, dialing 911. As the sound of screeching tires took off, many of the customers quickly got up and rushed toward the door. But, before they made it outside, the begging crackhead from the other day came in holding the bullet wound on his side.

"Suuumbody, call for help," he said, before dropping face first to the floor. Blood covered his white T-shirt and ran down on his dirty and greasy jeans.

Nate and I rushed to help the man. The others stood in shock, looking at the man who appeared to be fighting hard for his life. "Everybody get outside," Nate yelled. "Get these kids out of here and stop standin' around lookin'!"

Nate held the man in his arms, and I rushed outside looking down Union Boulevard to see if the police were coming. I called 911 again, this time telling the dispatcher that an ambulance was needed.

The policed arrived, then, ten minutes after that, an ambulance did. Five more minutes after that, the news reporters were pulling up, trying to get a story for the ten o'clock news. As soon as the police arrived, I became scarce. I didn't want anyone questioning me about anything, and the farther away from them I stayed, the better. Nate already knew the routine. The liquor store belonged to him, he didn't know nothing, and he didn't see nothing. Nobody was snitching, even though the majority of us had seen the gray 2004 Chevy Trailblazer that pulled away. I had the license plate number stuck in my head, but in my head it would stay.

From across the street, I leaned against the front of my laundromat, watching as the man who was shot was put into an ambulance. It looked as if he had a chance to survive, and if he did, maybe something of this magnitude would be a signal for him to clean up his act and get off the streets. Then, I saw two chicks who were in the store with their kids talking to a news reporter. This was their chance to make it big time like Antoine Dobson and they knew it. One straightened her lace-front wig that was tilted on her head, and the other kept yelling for her kids to move out of the way. The reporter loved every bit of having the two ghetto tricks on camera and she sucked it up.

"Tell us again what happened," the reporter said, preparing herself to switch the microphone to one of the chick's mouth. "Was he shot in or outside of the liquor store?"

The woman exaggerated, and did her best to get as much camera time as she could. "The dudes who shot him ran up in the liquor store like they were some kind of Mafia or somethin'. Da blasted the man right in the store and me and my babies were inside lookin' at everything that happened. Our kids were petrified and ain't no way they gon' sleep tonight after seein' somethin' like that. This mess is a shame and these nig . . . folks need to get it together."

"Damn right," the other chick said, nearly pushing the other one out of the way. "We can't even walk to the store with our kids without gettin' shot at. That bullet almost hit my daughter and it was this close to her head. A posse of them fools ran up in there, blasting bullets with masks coverin' da faces. We didn't get a good look at dem, but da were throwin' up gang signs and everythang."

I shook my damn head and had heard enough. But as soon as I was getting ready to go inside of the laundromat, a young black male reporter headed my way.

"Excuse me, sir," he said. "May I speak to you for a minute and ask you some questions?"

I hesitated, but pulled up my sagging cargo shorts and flattened my flowing waves with my hand. My black wife beater tightened around my chest, so I deemed myself as being appropriate for TV.

"I see you've been standing out here for a while," he said. "Did you see what happened today, or did you know the victim who was shot and is in critical condition?"

I cleared my throat as he held the mic close to my mouth. "No, I didn't see what happened, but I do go to P's laundromat and his liquor store across the street on Union Boulevard all the time. The laundromat dries my clothes for free and the environment is always calm, cool, and collected. The liquor store has some of the cheapest prices in town and—"

The reporter cut me off, as he suspected that the only thing I was interested in was promoting. "So, you didn't know the victim?"

"No, but I do know that the owner of the liquor store is a man who truly cares about this community. Sometimes he allows customers to get things on credit and if—"

"Thank you, sir," the reporter said, lowering his mic and walking off.

I guess I wasn't talking the nonsense he wanted to hear, so I went inside and looked across the street from afar. As I watched the charade continue outside, my cell phone vibrated. I looked at the flashing number, and seeing that it was Mama I answered.

"Prince, what are you doing on the news? What in the hell happened?"

"A man got shot and came into my store. I called the police."

"Is he gon' be all right?"

"I think so, but I'm not sure."

"Well, as long as you're okay, that's all I'm concerned about. You looked good on TV, too, and I called some of my girlfriends already and told them to watch the news. Those other two tricks, Lawd have mercy! They didn't make their mamas proud, and who in the hell told them to get in front of the cameras?"

"Don't know, Mama, but I need to go check on Nate to make sure he's okay. I'll hit you back later."

"Okay. But, when you come by tomorrow bring me a couple of beers and a carton of Virginia Slims."

"Did I say I was comin' by tomorrow? I may not make it until the weekend."

"Come on, Prince. I'm not gon' beg, but I'm over here having a nicotine fit. If you don't . . ."

"Enough said, Mama. Tomorrow. Now, I gotta go."

I hung up and went back outside to get a closer look at Nate, who was still being questioned by one of the officers. I was somewhat nervous, because I didn't

want the police to get after him over something he had
no control over. A long time ago, Nate had done time
in prison. He said that he'd been on the right track ever
since he'd been out, and I trusted his word. Still, I knew
the police had done a background check on him and
viewed him as nothing but a convicted felon. He was
so much more than just that and was truly a good man
who I was pleased to call my mentor. He was much better than that stupid motherfucker I knew as my father,
and I couldn't help but think about the night that I had
gone to his house to kill him.

*My partner, Cedric, and me sat in Romeo's car
waiting for my father, Derrick, to come home. I didn't
know if he was out with one of his many bitches that
night, or if he was at the pool hall with some of his
partners. Maybe he was at the strip club watching the
women shake their asses. I had seen him at the strip
club several weeks before, and we had words that
upset me more than they did him. I had even gone to
his house to borrow some money from him, but unbe-
knownst to me, that's the day I found out how much
that nigga hated me. He gave me fifty lousy dollars,
and pulled a gun out on me because I was disappointed in the amount. I'd needed some money to get
Romeo out of jail, and Derrick was my only option. As
I threw a fit, he threatened to kill me, and I threatened
to do the same. I was determined to get at him before
he got to me, so I waited for him that day. Just as I ran
out of assumptions about where he was, I watched the
nigga as he pulled into his driveway. Two cars were
behind him, and when I saw three men get out, that's
when I looked over at Cedric.*

*"Watch my back," I said. "If anybody look like they
want to jump, you know what to do."*

Cedric nodded and cocked his gun. Before the men went inside, I hurried out of the car and jogged across the street. My black hoodie was over my head and as I was dressed in all black, Derrick didn't even see me creeping up on him. I whispered his name and that's when his head snapped to the side.

I wasted no time pulling the gun from my pants, aiming it at him. "Good night, motherfucka. Sleep tight." The silencer fired off two shots that were quiet as a mouse. All Derrick's partners saw was his body drop to the hard concrete. Before they could pull out their guns, Cedric dropped one of the men from a distance. The other stood with his hands held up high and away from Derricks's body. Sweat laced his forehead and he didn't know what to say.

I removed the hoodie from my head. "Do you know who I am?" I asked.

He squinted and slowly nodded. "You Derrick's son, ain't you?"

I was trigger happy, and little did the man know, he had the wrong answer. "Wrong answer. I'm nobody you should know. Do I need to try this again?"

I was getting ready to unload on his ass, but he begged me not to. "You're right. I . . . I don't know you and I've never seen you before in my life. Let me live, man, and I swear there won't be no beef between me and you."

I turned my gun sideways, frowning and high as hell. "Nigga, I don't trust you. You—"

"But you can," he rushed to say. "You can trust me. I'll give you anything you want and nobody will ever know what happened here."

"What I want is what's due to me. Eighteen years of back pay, and the sooner you figure out what that is, the better off you'll be."

*Cedric walked up to me. "Man, why you out here negotiating with this fool? Kill his ass and let's go."*

*"No," the man said in a shaky voice. "I can take care of that for you. Just give me until tomorrow and you'll be set for life."*

*I told Cedric to hold his gun steady on the man and asked Cedric for his cell phone. He gave it to me, then lifted his gun where the red razor light was aimed at the man's forehead. I gave the man my gun and told him to shoot Derrick again.*

*"Why?" he asked.*

*"Evidence. If you cross me, I'll have proof that you did this, not me."*

*The man hesitated, but shot off two more bullets that tore holes into Derrick's chest. I took my pictures, and the man quickly handed the gun back to me.*

*Cedric lowered his gun, unclear about what I was doing.*

*"Meet me downtown tomorrow by the riverboats at noon," I said. "Have my money and you never have to see my face again."*

*The man nodded and Cedric and I ran to get into the car. I sped off and he couldn't wait to ask.*

*"That cat Derrick was yo' old dude?"*

*I nodded, feeling not an ounce of lost love for him.*

*"Daaaamn. I thought I was ruthless, but you did that shit with no remorse. From what I know, he got a lot of connections, Prince, and I hope that shit don't come back to haunt you."*

*I shrugged, not really giving a care, but hoping that his friend wouldn't cross me.*

*The next day, his friend met up with me, giving me $300,000. I thought it would go a long way, but my*

*friend Cedric had snaked me, causing much of that*
*money to slip away. He had me set up, and unfortu-*
*nately, he didn't live much longer after that. I had no*
*tolerance for people who fucked me, and father or not,*
*Derrick deserved to die by the hands of his own son.*

I continued to look across the street, but I was sure
Nate knew how to handle himself under pressure.
It appeared as if he had everything under control. I
leaned against the glass windows with my hands in my
pockets, keeping my eyes on things. Many people were
still hanging out, trying to see what was going on. I was
so involved until I got a whiff of sweet perfume that
tickled my nose. When I turned my head, I saw Poetry
standing very close by while talking to another chick.
This time, Poetry rocked thigh-high jean shorts that
revealed her shapely, tall legs. A pair of wood platform
heels with turquoise, yellow, and pink flowers on them
covered her feet, exposing her manicured toenails.
An off-the-shoulder pink shirt cut at her midriff and
stretched around her tiny breasts. Her short cut was
neatly lined and her makeup and eyelashes were on
like a work of art. I stared at her just for a moment, giving her the attention she truly deserved. When I turned
my attention back to the scene of the crime, that's when
she sashayed by without saying a word to me. She was
with an older woman who wobbled by with a cane. I
could see some striking resemblances and I noticed
them laughing and talking a lot. The older woman put
some clothes in the dryer, and they both sat down to
talk. Realizing that Poetry must have driven her rela-
tive there to dry some clothes, I jogged across the street
and waited until the last police car left, which was only
a few minutes later. With my hands sunk into my pockets, I went inside of the liquor store to check on Nate.

"Everything cool?" I asked as he stood folding his arms.

"Yeah, it's fine. I just hate bein' questioned by them mothersuckas. They always tryin' to make you feel guilty about somethin' you ain't have nothin' to do with. We good, though, so no worries."

I looked down at the bloodstained floor, shaking my head. "I hope ol' boy gon' be okay. He seemed like a fighter. I was surprised the ambulance got here so soon."

"Yeah, me too. I think he gon' make it and I hope he stay away from here with all that damn beggin' he be doin'. Some people don't like that shit, and those fools who shot him betta not come by here again. I see those fools runnin' through here all the time. They know better than to spray bullets around here, especially with those kids around."

"Kids around or not, those niggas do not care. I'm just glad nobody else was hurt. That kind of mess can hurt business."

"I agree. But today is today, and all we can do is look forward to tomorrow. Now let's get this place closed and cleaned up. Besides, it's gettin' late. I got myself a date tonight."

"With who?" I laughed. "And whoever she is, I hope you don't run out here sportin' those bibs and Stacys. You gotta look fly for the ladies. Even I know that."

Nate looked at my black Air Jordans that had red untied shoelaces. My cargo shorts weren't all that clean and my wife beater made me look simple. "You need not tell me how to dress, lookin' like that. Those young gals might like all those muscles and thug shit you got goin' on, but real women ain't down with that. I'm sure yo' mama is goin' to love me in my bibs tonight."

Nate laughed, and I knew he was joking about being with Mama, as he had done so many times in the past. I tried to hook the two of them up on the side, but Mama wasn't having it. I guess Nate was too nice for her, and Raylo seemed to have her on lock, especially since the last beat-down she'd caught for cheating on him.

Almost an hour later, Nate and I had finished cleaning the floor. He locked up, then headed upstairs to his apartment to get dressed for his date. I went back to the laundromat, and since it was almost eleven o'clock, I reminded the people inside that I'd be closing in an hour. It angered me when I'd see people strolling in at five minutes to midnight, trying to wash their clothes. Sometimes I didn't mind staying, but if the sign on the door said OPEN UNTIL MIDNIGHT, then why not come earlier? Either way, it had been a long day and I wasn't staying any longer than I had to tonight. I had already started to tidy up, and when I looked around to see if Poetry and the older woman were still there, I noticed they were gone.

The floor was filthy, so I got my mop from the closet and started to clean the floor. There were three ladies left inside, and one brotha who was helping his woman fold some clothes. They were talking about what had happened earlier and were watching the updates on the late-night news. As I strolled by with the mop, one of the ladies asked if I had change for fifty dollars.

"Your machine doesn't change fifties and it's all I got," she said.

I reached in my pocket, then counted out the change to her. As I was doing so, I looked up and saw Poetry come back inside. This time, she walked over to the other woman to converse with her.

"Thanks," the woman said. "I'm almost done, and I shouldn't be much longer."

All I did was nod and continued to mop the floor. I purposely ignored Poetry, who laughed a bit, talked louder, and even stood right next to me, getting a soda as I cleaned the floor. Once I was done, I returned the mop to the closet and went into my office. I called to check on Mama, but got no answer. Then I called to see what Francine was up to, since I told her I'd see her later. She didn't answer either, so I pulled a crossword puzzle book from my desk and started to work it.

Watching the clock tick away, at five minutes to midnight, I got up to see if anyone was still there. The only person I saw was the brotha who had been folding his clothes, but he was on his way out. With a cart in front of him, he rolled it out the door.

"I'll bring this back in," he shouted so I could hear him. "So, don't lock the door."

I walked toward the front door, watching as the brotha loaded his clothes in the car. He returned the cart and I took it from him at the door.

"Thanks," I said and he walked off.

I was tired as hell and seriously needed some rest from being up all night. I locked the door, and pushed the cart alongside the others. Surprisingly, when I looked to my far right, Poetry sat with her legs crossed and a newspaper in front of her.

"We're closed," I said.

She lowered the newspaper to her lap, and looked at the round clock on the wall. "Last time I checked, you closed at midnight. I still have two minutes."

In no mood for her tonight, I ignored her and went back to my office. Routinely, I removed my Glock from my drawer, tucking it inside of my pants. Then, I checked the back door to make sure it was locked, secured my supply closet and, after grabbing my keys off my desk, I closed the door to my office. I turned off the

TV and the lights followed thereafter. The streetlight outside was the only thing that gave off light.

"Daang," Poetry said, standing up. She walked toward the door where I was. "How am I supposed to see what I'm reading?"

"Take the paper with you because we're officially closed."

She placed the newspaper in one of the chairs. "No, that's okay. I didn't come in here to read anyway. I came to ask you for a job."

"I'm not hiring."

She shrugged. "Maybe not, but I see a whole lot of things around here that need to be done."

"Whatever those things are, they'll eventually get done by me. So I'll say it again . . . Not hiring."

She folded her arms. "Okay, but why haven't you called me? You say I'm too ghetto for you, but I digress."

"I haven't called because I don't have your number. Just in case you forgot, it's in the trash. As for the ghetto thing . . . yeah, whatever, ma. You know what's up."

I unlocked the door, opening it so we could walk out together. Poetry didn't move. She tapped her foot on the floor and glared at me.

"What is it?" I said, somewhat irritated. I was ready to go chill, and was in no mood to be catching attitude from a chick who didn't seem to have nothing else better to do with her time than harass me.

"What's with you, Prince? Why you all funny acting and didn't I apologize for calling you a thief? Then, I was nice enough to give your money back, and not once did you thank me for doing that. I gave you my number so we could be friends, and when I saw you on the news today, I came down here to see if we could squash what happened and start fresh. Now, if you ain't down with that, say so."

I looked her over, still unsatisfied with her comment and attitude. I pushed the door open, and gestured for her to walk out. "No, I'm not down with us bein' friends. But if you want a quickie or some sex, I'm always down with that. Friends and relationships, sorry, not for me."

"Umph. Too bad because I don't have sex with assholes. I am still interested in a job, though, and just so you know, I don't give up too easily when I feel as though something is within my reach."

"An asshole would apply to me, so don't waste your time. Now, good night."

She rolled her eyes to the top of her head, then made her way out the door. Saying nothing else to me, she walked down the street and got into her car, which was the last one parked on the street.

After she sped off, I locked the front door and made my way upstairs to my apartment. The last thing I needed right now was a chick with hassles. My history with women wasn't that great. Never again would I get attached to any chick, and as fine as Poetry was, her looks weren't enough to move me. She didn't seem like the kind of gal who would be interested in becoming one of my fuck buddies, so getting with her on any other level was a wrap. I couldn't see the purpose, but maybe I wasn't looking for it.

# Chapter Four

## Wake Up, Before It's Too Late . . .

I crawled out of bed, still feeling beat as ever. Maybe because I stayed up nearly all night playing Xbox Live and lifting weights. Should've been out clubbing, but after all that had happened in my life, I was doing my best to keep things low-key. The streets wasn't nothing to play with, and I had learned some valuable lessons along the way. Sometimes I felt as if my life was boring, then I was grateful that I wasn't either dead or in jail. I had definitely been on that path, but something pulled me back. I was afraid that retaliation would be ordered for killing three niggas in a lounge that day, or the police would come looking for me. It hadn't happened as of yet, and to be honest, I was living day by day. Each day, though, I was trying to get focused. If I made it through that mess, and was still alive, I had to consider it a blessing. There was no other way to look at it. And as worried as I was about what would happen to me, so were many others. Mama kept saying that she was having dreams about me dying, and my half sister, Patrice, used to call every day to check on me. Once things calmed down, she packed her bags and jetted to California. I didn't think her leaving had much to do with her worries for me, though, and I figured that as soon as her mother died, Patrice would leave St. Louis. She did, and I hadn't heard from her since.

I showered, put on my Nike basketball shorts and a white loose T-shirt. While looking in the mirror, I brushed my waves and put some Vaseline on my dry lips. After I put on my socks, I slid my feet into my Nike sandals. I hurried downstairs to open the laundromat, then got on my way to Mama's house so I could take her the cigarettes and beer she'd asked for. It was only seven o'clock in the morning, but the sun was baking my body in the car like it was an oven. I couldn't wait for the air to crank up and I had it on full blast. Drake was spilling his lyrics through my speakers and I zoomed down Natural Bridge Boulevard feeling upbeat.

When I arrived at Mama's house, I saw Raylo's car parked in the driveway. I knew it was too early for either of them to be awake, so instead of knocking on the door, I used my key to go inside. As soon as I opened the door, I saw Raylo lying on the living room couch with a sheet covering him. The TV was loud and a bottle of Jack Daniels was on the coffee table. He was snoring so loudly that he didn't hear me come in. I crept into the kitchen, putting the bag on the table and leaving it there so Mama could see it. I figured she was asleep in her room, so I headed back to the front door so I could leave.

"Wait a minute," Raylo said, clearing his throat and slowly sitting up on the couch. "Don't leave yet, Prince. I need to get at you 'bout somethin'."

I moved closer to the couch and folded my arms. "What's up?"

Raylo cleared his throat again, then cracked the bottle of Jack Daniels to help whatever was in his throat go down. "Ahhhh," he said, slamming the bottle back on the table. "Better."

I looked at my watch, as Raylo seemed to be stalling and I didn't have time. I had to get back to the laundromat to remove my change from the machines, before it got too crowded.

"I wanted to know if I could get a loan," Raylo said. "Things gettin' kind of tight around here. Me and yo' mama ain't got it like we used to."

"I already gave Mama some money. If you need some, why don't you just ask her?"

"Because she ain't here right now. She left yesterday and told me she would be back later. I'm sure she'll be back later today or tomorrow, but even when she does come back, she don't have the kind of money I need right now. If you let me hold 'bout ten Gs, I'll be sure to get it back to you as soon as I can."

I hesitated, only because Raylo had never done much for me. He'd been in my life since I was eleven years old, and all I ever saw him do was drink, smoke weed, cheat on my mother, and kick her ass. I knew Mama loved him, though, but I didn't feel right giving his ass no money. I also knew that if Mama needed it, she would ask. She never had any problems asking me for anything, and if the ten Gs weren't going to benefit her, then my answer was a big fat no.

"Man, things kind of tight, and I ain't got that kind of money right now. If you would have said a couple of hundred, maybe. But ten Gs is a lot for me to give up."

Raylo's face twisted, just that fast. "Nigga, you know you got it. I said I'd give it back. I got myself in a li'l jam that I need to get out of. I thought we were like family and I really ain't got no other place to turn right now."

I stretched, then yawned. "I repeat; I ain't got it right now. And even if I did, I'm not sure if I'd want to help you with your so-called jam. Tryin' to save my dollars, and if I keep on givin' when I ain't got, then I'll be without. Tell Mama to hit me up later. I gotta go."

"You's a stingy-ass motherfucka, Prince. I've taken care of you since you were ten or eleven and when yo' whack-ass daddy didn't want shit to do with you, I stepped in. I have never asked your punk ass for nothin' and now that you keepin' a li'l change in yo' pockets, you actin' all high and mighty like you can't help a nigga who paved the way for you. That's some cold shit, bruh, but I'm not gon' kiss yo' ass. Just remember that you may need me one day. I'm gon' turn my back on you, like you just did me."

My eyes shot daggers at Raylo, because he was a damn liar, claiming he paved the way for me. How? I wanted to cuss his ass out, but realized he wasn't worth my time. Just like my deadbeat father, Raylo wasn't nothing to me. If anything, taking his path would have led me straight to hell. I wasn't trying to go there. Instead of saying all of that, I snickered and shook my head before walking away. Raylo hated when people didn't stoop to his level, and ignoring him was always the wrong route to take. Before my hand touched the doorknob, he already had the back of my shirt gripped in his hand. He shoved me toward the living room so hard that I almost fell. Weighing every bit of 180 pounds, I could never go toe-to-toe with Raylo, who was nearly twice my size. My Glock could but, unfortunately for me, it was in my car.

"Man, I'm not goin' here with you today," I said, shaking off my anger and taking a few steps toward the door.

He shoved me back again, then pointed his finger at me. "Don't you walk away from me when I'm speakin' to you, nigga! You ain't that damn grown, and who in the hell do you think you are, talkin' to me like I ain't shit? I will kick yo' ass, boy, then call the police to tell them you broke into my house! And when I tell them you were the one who killed—"

Threatening to snitch on me was not the direction to take. My forehead swelled with wrinkles and my teeth gritted. "You do what you have to do, punk! But remember, yo' rap sheet is much longer than mine. I got mega shit on you, too, so you'd better think twice about what you're sayin'. Now, I got work to do. Somethin' you haven't known about in years. Get the fuck out of my way, and if a fight is what you're lookin' for this mornin', I ain't got time for it!"

I stepped forward again, and Raylo took his fist, slamming it into my gut. Pain rushed through my midsection, causing me to double over before staggering and dropping to one knee. I held my stomach, unable to regroup after such a hard blow. I tightened my eyes, wondering how in the hell Mama could bear his punches after so many years.

"If you rush up, it better be to make yo' way to the door. If you move in my direction, this will be the last time you will ever see light," he threatened.

I didn't doubt Raylo's words one bit. And even when I tried to move, my stomach was so sore that all I could do was continue to soothe it with my hand. Staying in the same position with my head down, I wasn't about to challenge Raylo. I knew I couldn't take him with my bare hands, and my strength was nowhere near what it used to be. He stood for a second, waiting for me to make my move. When I didn't, he headed toward the back. Doing the norm, he went into Mama's bedroom and slammed the door. That's when I slowly eased up.

"Shit," I said, as my stomach hurt even more when I stood straight up. I surely thought about going to my car to get my gun, but the last thing I wanted was for the police to be on the scene. Instead, I slowly walked to my car and dropped back on the seat for a while. I was sure Raylo would tell Mama what happened, and

I awaited her call to ask me what I had done to him. Then again, lately she'd been siding with me. But even if I thought this was enough to make her throw him out on his ass, I was positive that wouldn't happen. After all of the beatings, why not? I couldn't help but to sit and think about the many times I'd seen him go upside her head, and what I'd seen him do about a month ago to a woman who was standing on Newstead Avenue. He didn't see me, but I parked my car and rolled down my window to hear what was up that day.

*Raylo had the frail redbone chick who looked to be in her thirties by the back of her hair. His grip was so tight that tears were pouring down her face and her eyes were squeezed together. She kept begging him to let go.*

*"Baby, please," she said, trying to laugh it off, but appeared to be in so much pain. "I won't do it again. I promise. Ju . . . just give me another chance, Sugar Bear."*

*I guessed she thought that calling him a pet name would help ease her pain, but she must not have known Raylo like I did. "You slutty bitch," he said, then pushed her down where she skinned her knees. They were bloody as ever, and he picked her up, again, dragging her to the side of a building like a ragdoll. He lifted his hand that had four thick gold rings on each finger, slapping her so hard her head snapped to the side, as if she were in a heavyweight fight getting her ass beat by Mike Tyson. Raylo spat in her face as he spoke, then squeezed her nose, trying to break it away from her face. Blood ran from her nose and dripped over her lips to her shaky chin. The woman's ear-ringing screams could have woken up the whole neighborhood but, unfortunately, no one stopped to help, including myself.*

His fist tore into her stomach that day, just as it had done mine. It sickened me to watch what he had done to that woman, and she was in the same predicament as Mama. Raylo would apologize for his abuse, and all would be good, until he was ready for some more gangsta shit again. Knowing so, I drove off, thinking what a gotdamn shame this truly was.

I arrived at the laundromat a little after eight. There were already several people inside, but I started to remove the quarters from the machine. My face was still scrunched up, thinking about Raylo putting his hands on me and getting away with it. There was a time I would never allow something like that to happen, but trouble was the last thing I needed. Whenever I felt like I wanted to do something that would bring trouble my way, all I had to do was sit down and read some of the letters I'd gotten from my partner Romeo who was in jail. His letters were so damn depressing. All he wanted was out. He'd been thrown in the hole for fighting, stabbed, and he and the guards didn't get along. I wished like hell that I could help him, but there wasn't a damn thing I could do with him being behind bars for the next thirty-something years. All I could do was send him encouraging words and keep the money flowing.

Once I emptied the coins from each machine, I went back to my office to put the change in coin holders so I could take them to the bank. The laundromat business was a good business to get into, and more than anything, it kept me doing something positive. My liquor store made double . . . triple the money the laundromat did, and with Nate being friendly to my customers, that always kept them coming back to support. I still had some work to do with my attitude, but the thing was, people had to wash clothes and couldn't care less about who I was or what I was doing here. As far as they knew, I was working for a white man who was paying me to run his business. And if ever asked, that's exactly what I would say because, for whatever dumbass reason, many black people supported white businesses before they did a black business.

I had stacks of quarters on my desk and was taking my time as I put them in the coin holders. "My Beats" by Dr. Dre headphones were on my ears, drowning out the ladies conversing and laughing with each other while washing. I couldn't hear a thing, but when I looked up, Poetry was standing on the other side of the door. She had the same shorts on that she had on last night but with a different top. I really wasn't up for her mouth today, but I was sure the blank expression on my face meant nothing to her. I removed the headphones from my ears, placing them on my desk.

"Sorry to bother you," she said. "But, do you have a minute or two to spare?"

I shrugged, not saying if I did or didn't.

"First, I wanted to apologize to you, again, for coming off like I did. It's just that that man made me mad for putting his hands on that woman, and I really felt as if you should have done something. A part of me was madder at you than I was at him, and I was wrong for going off on you like I did. I tried to make peace with the situation by offering you my number, but you know what happened with that. Yesterday, I tried again, but my attempts have failed. This is my last time coming to you like this, and I'm not going to keep making a fool of myself for someone who acts like they really don't care."

I shrugged. "I'm still not giving you a job, and the truth is, I really don't care, Poetry. I don't know what you want from me, and what's done is done. You gave

me back my hundred dollars, so what's the big deal? I
don't get this, ma, and if I say that your apology is ac-
cepted, don't keep sweatin' me, all right? That's unless
you want somethin' else from me. If so, you need to tell
me what it is, because I'm confused as hell about you
showin' up here all the time. I get a feelin' that it's to
harass me, but like I said last night, you're wastin' your
time."

She tried to remain calm, but couldn't help herself.
Her hand went up to her hip and her previously nice
tone changed. "Are you kidding me? I don't have to
harass no one. I was just trying to be nice, but I see you
wish to continue insulting me for no reason. Maybe I
am wasting my time, but something was placed on my
heart to do the right thing. As for the job, fuck it! Forget
I ever asked."

"I will. You've done the right thing and I appreciate
it. Now, if you don't mind, I have work to do. I need
to get to the bank before noon, and if I don't get done
countin' this change, I'll never make it. So, see you
around and have a good day."

Poetry sucked in her bottom lip and turned to leave.
I got back to counting my change, and no sooner had
I picked up the headphones, than she appeared at the
door again.

"One more thing," she said. "Don't flatter yourself
thinking you're all that, because you're not. You're
handsome and everything, but I've seen and have had
better. Your attitude stinks and you're probably one of
those down-low brothas who don't know or recognize a
good thing when he sees it."

I swore this chick was crazy. If she was trying to win
me over, or get a job, this wasn't the way to do it. Having enough, I stood up and lowered my loose basketball
shorts to my knees. My dick plopped out and I lifted my
shirt, revealing my abs too.

"Close the door and let me show you how down low I am. Low down and dirty, some may say, but never on the down low. You said it was my loss if I didn't want to go there with you, and to be honest with you, Poetry, I don't. You're not my type, I don't need nobody working for me, but if you're anxious to get some dick up in you, again, I can help just about any woman with that."

Poetry scanned my body, stopping at my hanging muscle. "I disagree. With a dick that little, I don't think you can help, nor satisfy any woman with what you got. I'm out."

She walked away again, this time leaving me with a bruised ego. I was the first to admit that I didn't have a mammoth-sized dick, but it was definitely something I could work with. The previous chicks in my life had no complaints, so I looked down at my goods and brushed off her comment. I raised my shorts and got back to counting my change.

By noon, I headed to the bank to deposit my money. I dialed out to call Mama on the way there, but Raylo answered the phone.

"Is my mama there?" I asked.

"Hell no," he said, then hung up.

I called her cell phone, and when she didn't answer, I left a message for her to call me.

Nearly three days had elapsed and I still hadn't heard from Mama. I was somewhat worried, but she was known for disappearing, then showing up weeks later. It had been such a long time since she'd done that, and since we'd been talking almost every other day, I felt as if her disappearing days were behind us. I stocked the shelves behind the counter at the liquor store while leaving her a message.

"Uh, Miss Lady, where in the hell are you at? You could call me to say what's up and I want to know if you got your cigs and beer. I know Raylo probably told you what went down and I hope you ain't upset with me about that shit. If you need somethin' you need to let me know. I'd rather give what I got to you, not to him. Ya feel me? Anyhow, get at me soon, all right?"

I ended the call and got back to stocking the shelves. Once I was finished, I stood behind the counter with Nate. The store had been flooded with customers, and he was mad at me for announcing on the news that we gave things away on credit.

"You shouldn't have ever said that shit," Nate said. "These fools been runnin' up in here like crazy, tryin' to get somethin' for free. I had to put up a cardboard sign that says IF YOU AIN'T GOT MONEY TO PAY, YOU WON'T BE SERVED."

Nate pointed to the sign in the corner that I hadn't seen. I laughed and apologized for my inappropriate way to generate more business.

"I know you meant no harm, so I ain't trippin'," he said. "Next time, take out a business ad in the newspaper or somethin'. You may have more luck."

I laughed and helped Nate knock out some of the customers. When Jenay came in hugged up with one of her women, I waited on them too. I had a slick grin on my face, as getting to know them both on a much more personal level was interesting, as well as entertaining.

"What can I get you?" I asked her.

"You always know the right thing to give me, but I'll take a pack of Newports, a gallon of milk, and a box of condoms."

All I did was blush, and retrieved the items Jenay asked me to get. I gave her the total and she paid me. As I gave the items to her, she left the condoms on the tray. "Those are yours," she said. "Bring them with you later. *We* hope to see you around . . . let's say, ten?"

I winked. "Sure."

Jenay and her companion walked away. I was all smiles, until Nate smacked me on the back of my neck. "Get yo' mind out of the gutter. And how in the hell can you get invited into her bedroom and I've been tryin' to hit that shit for years?"

"'Cause you ain't got it like me, Nate. I told you those bibs ain't no winner and you don't believe me. You need to let me hook you up, then you may be able to slide into them sheets like I be doin'."

Nate laughed and brushed off my comment. "Whatever, fool. You will never get me in that shit you be wearin'. I don't care if Jenay looks like Lola Falana or not, I'm stickin' with my style."

"Who in the fuck is Lola Falana? She must be ancient, 'cause I ain't never heard of her."

"She is one of the finest black women that ever walked this earth. And every time I see Jenay, I have dreams about her. If you dippin' into that, you are one lucky-ass Negro."

I shrugged, not really feeling lucky at all. As far as I saw it, it was just some pussy. Wasn't sure if I was up to sex tonight, had other shit on my mind. Plus, it was the Fourth of July weekend. I had no desire to stay cooped up in my apartment, and Nate and I talked about going downtown on the St. Louis Riverfront, Fair St. Louis, to watch the fireworks. It was a yearly tradition and not too many folks in St. Louis missed out.

Nate and I decided to close the liquor store around six o'clock, so we could make it to Fair St. Louis before everything popped off. Since it was so damn hot outside, I changed into my white wife beater, cocked a cap to the side to shield the sun, and sported my shades.

Nate left the bibs at home, and settled for a pair of jean shorts, a T-shirt, and leather sandals. He knew better than to look like a damn fool with me, and as we rode the crowded Metrolink to downtown, he laughed about changing it up a bit.

"I didn't want to hear your mouth, but don't you ever think I'ma put my bibs away for you."

"Ay, keep 'em. Don't matter to me, but when the ladies don't show you no love, don't be mad at me."

"I get love all the time, no matter what I wear. I keep tellin' you that clothes don't make a man. You'd better learn somethin'."

"I feel you, no doubt. And you know I respect all the advice that you've ever given me."

Nate nodded and looked ahead as we stood, holding on to the rail above so we wouldn't fall. The Metrolink was getting more packed with each stop, and everyone had to squeeze in. When we reached the Arch grounds by the Riverfront, many got off. Nate and I headed toward the Arch, where many of the festivities took place.

"With all that's going on around in St. Louis," Nate said, "and with brothaman gettin' shot the other day by the liquor store, are you sure you want to hang around in the Lou? I mean, a young man like you should have some plans . . . big plans. I hope you've been thinkin' about your future."

"I have, but when I do think about it, I see it right here. I'm not runnin' from nothin' around here, and nothin' surprises me at all. I've seen plenty of niggas lose their lives and die right in front of me. I've seen it all, Nate, and this is the way of life, ain't it?"

"Not necessarily," Nate replied. He turned his head as two chicks with very short shorts on walked by. He licked his lips and shook his head. "Did you see that gash on that skeeza? Umph, umph, umph!" He looked again, then got back to his conversation with me. "What you've been around and what you're accustomed to ain't always the way life is supposed to be. I like your style, Prince, and I like how you distance yourself from all of these hatin' niggas around here. I know that comes from all that you've been through, and you've got a good head on your shoulders. Just keep that attitude you got. You'll see what else life has out here to offer you. It ain't necessarily what you've seen, it's what you haven't had an opportunity to see yet."

"I get that," I said, stopping at a vender's booth to get a turkey leg. I hadn't eaten all day and was starving. "Do you want one?"

"Nah, I'ma get me some funnel cake and one of those Chicago-style hotdogs they be havin'. I'll wait."

We stood in the long line, waiting to get my turkey leg. I truly did understand what Nate was saying, but St. Louis was the only home I'd known and would probably be where I would be forever. Besides, Mama was here and I couldn't see myself ever leaving her. I paid for my turkey leg and we continued to talk, walk, and look at every pretty chick who swaggered by. There were plenty of them to see and many were showing all skin. The fair consisted of people from all races and backgrounds, as this was a time that everyone in the Lou seemed to come together.

Once Nate got his funnel cake and hotdog, we found a spot on the stairs of the Gateway Arch to watch the fireworks. Horse carriages rode by and many vendors were selling balloons and unique lights to those passing by. I couldn't help but think of my son, wondering what he was up to and where he was now living. He was almost two years old by now, and it bothered me that there was a possibility he might not ever get to know me. I remembered the first time Nadine told me she was pregnant. I denied him, wanting nothing to do with him at all. I guessed this was payback for my neglect, and payback for taking matters into my own hands after she was killed. Her mother called me an animal that day, and she blamed me for Nadine being killed. It was hard for me to live with that, only because I knew there was so much truth behind it. Those niggas were after me and, unfortunately, Nadine was in the car with me. I shut my eyes, thinking about a horrible day that would haunt me forever.

*We were riding in my car that day. I was teasing Nadine about her new boyfriend and she playfully shoved my shoulder. When we got to a stoplight, she turned her head to look out of the partially lowered window. I looked in her direction too, and when a burgundy Regal pulled up beside us, my eyes stayed focused like a laser. The rear window slowly lowered and I saw the tip of an AK-47 aim in our direction. My foot hit the accelerator, but because of the wet pavement, all I heard were my wheels turning in circles, burning rubber. I yelled for Nadine to duck, and she dropped down on the front seat, yelling and screaming.*

*"My baby!" she said, wanting to protect our son, who was strapped in a car seat on the back seat, between two laundry baskets. "I gotta get my baby!"*

*As the bullets hit against my car, it sounded like a Fourth of July celebration going on. Glass was shattered everywhere, and as fast as I was driving, the car beside us kept up. Nadine jumped up from the seat, shouting for her baby and trying to protect him. When her body jerked forward, I knew she had been hit by flying bullets. I slammed on the brakes, doing a spinning U-turn in the middle of the street that left my car smoking. Nadine's body fell backward, slamming into the dash and plopping down on the seat.*

"*Shit!*" *I shouted. I nervously touched her chest, trying to see if she was still breathing.*

*I couldn't believe this shit was happening, and as the other car sped away, I panicked, driving like a bat out of hell to get to Barnes Hospital, which was less than a mile away.*

"*Nadine!*" *I kept yelling, trying to get a response.* "*Get up!*" *By now, the whites of her eyes were showing and she had no response. From what I could see in the rearview mirror, Prince Jr. was okay. He sat quietly on the back seat and I was thankful that the laundry baskets were on both sides of him. My breathing was getting heavier and heavier, my legs were shaking, and my sweaty palms were so slippery I could barely keep my hands on the steering wheel. When I reached the hospital, I put the car in park and carried Nadine's limp body into the emergency room.*

"*Help me!*" *I yelled at the nurses and doctors on duty.* "*Somebody please help me!*"

*Help arrived, but it was too late for Nadine.*

I couldn't get the thoughts of her out of my head and if it had not been for me, taking it upon myself to kill my partner Cedric, Nadine very well could still be alive. That's just something I had to live with, and living with it damn sure wasn't easy.

Nate waved his hand in front of my face. "Wake up," he said. "Are you there?"

I blinked and wiped my tired eyes. "Yeah, I'm here. Just thinkin' about some stuff, that's all."

He squeezed my shoulder and patted me twice on the back. "Don't be so serious all the time. You're still young, Prince, and you need to enjoy life. Have some fun. Leave what has happened to you in the past. If I hung on to all that's happened to me, I would be one sick motherfucka."

"Nate, why haven't you moved on and done somethin' different? I know that workin' at a liquor store ain't the limit of your dreams, is it? I mean, you seem like a smart man who is capable of doin' anything you want to."

Nate took the last bite of his hotdog, then squeezed the wrapper in his hand. "I had big dreams, like you did in high school. Got a basketball scholarship and my first year in college I fucked up. Started partying all the time, hangin' out with my friends and fuckin' any and everything in sight. Got caught up one day with some friends who decided to jump on this brotha who hollered at his girlfriend. I sat in the car while they beat that Negro's ass, and when all was said and done, he died. They hit me up with a manslaughter charge and the life that I had known was over. I got twenty-five years, just like that, over a bitch that wasn't even mine. That's why you must watch the company you keep and know who your friends are, more than you know your enemies. Since then, I just live day-by-day, appreciatin' my freedom and knowin' that things could have been a lot worse. I'm too old to talk about startin' over, but you have your whole life ahead of you. Make wise decisions, and your life will go a long way."

"I couldn't agree with you more, and havin' your mind all wrapped around women can sholl fuck up some things. That's why I keep my distance. I've seen too many niggas fuck they lives up over some pussy."

Nate laughed while eyeing several more women who walked by. "It's a powerful thing," he said. "And even though there are some straight nutcrackers out there, you will find some women who will genuinely have your back. While in prison, I saw some women straight holdin' it down for their men, no matter what. The gal I was with moved the fuck on after two months. I haven't heard from her since. I didn't expect her to remain loyal to me, but after four years together, one simple letter would have suited me just fine. I got nothin'."

I couldn't help but think about Romeo and all that he was going through. His and Nate's situations sounded so similar. I was so sure that plenty of other brothas in prison could tell the same story. Wrong place, wrong friends, wrong time. "How . . . how was it in prison, Nate? Is everything they say about it really true? I mean, I know it ain't no picnic, but is it as bad as many people make it out to be?"

Nate looked me straight in my eyes. "You don't really know, unless you've been there. And trust me when I say it is no place that any man on this earth would want to be, especially young men. Everything that you hear is true; then there comes a side that many of us rather not tell. It's horrible, Prince, and I wouldn't wish prison life on my worst damn enemy. I'll leave it there."

I guess that was the first time anyone had ever put it out there like that for me, and I understood why Romeo never wanted to discuss what was going on with him, nor the specifics. I put the thoughts to the back of my mind, and that was easy to do when I saw Poetry walking down the street with a freckle-faced dude next to her. He seemed much older than she was and had on some nerdy-ass glasses. His cap was pulled down on his head, almost covering his eyes. They both were eating ice cream and she looked giddy as ever as they talked. I had to go fuck with her, only because she'd been fucking with me.

"I'll be right back," I said to Nate as I hurried down the steps to catch up with Poetry and her man. When I did, I crept up from behind and tapped her shoulder. "Ay," I said, causing her to quickly turn around. "Don't I know you from somewhere?"

She looked at the brotha next to her, then shrugged her shoulder. "No, I don't think so. You don't look familiar to me, so I think you may have the wrong person."

"I don't think so, because there couldn't be another chick on this planet as fine as you are. Your name is Poetry, right?"

The dude she was with folded his arms and looked at Poetry, who seemed tongue-tied. "That's my name, but I don't know you, all right? Now, if you don't mind, I'd like to get back to my walk."

"Sure." I smiled. "Go right ahead. I just happened to find your phone number you gave me the other day, and I had hoped to call you real soon. But if you're kickin' it with ol' boy, then I don't want to waste my time."

This time, the brotha she was with sighed. "Can we go now?" he said. "I want to find somewhere close to sit."

"Yes, we must do so," she said to the brotha, then looked at me and cut her eyes before walking off.

I chuckled, thinking what a joke some women were. There she was pursuing the hell out of me when all along she had a man. I guess he wasn't fulfilling her needs, and any man who put up with that mouth of hers was courageous.

I went back to where Nate was and we talked to each other until the fireworks got started. The Arch grounds had gotten even more crowded and police were everywhere, trying to make sure everything stayed in order. They could only do so much, and as soon as the eardrum-busting fireworks were over, two fights broke out. One was a group of white boys who had gotten drunk and started calling each other names, and the other was a group of girls who were pulling each other's hair out. As we moved with the crowd, that's when we saw a group of black men starting to yell at each other. Too bad the man next to us referred to them as niggers, and after all of the advice Nate had given me, he almost lost it.

"What in the fuck did you just say?" Nate said to the elderly white man who seemed shaken by the pitch of Nate's voice, as well as his intimidating look.

The man lowered his head and tried to abruptly walk away, but couldn't because the crowd wasn't moving fast enough.

"You dumbass fool," Nate shouted, walking so close to the man that he was stepping on the back of his shoes. "You down here with all these people and let somethin' that ignorant slip from your mouth. I should beat yo' ass for bein' so stupid!"

"Leave that old man alone," another man shouted.

Nate's fist tightened and I had to grab his arm to stop him from landing it somewhere. "Nate!" I said. "Chill! Damn, man, you down here preachin' to me about doin' the right thing and you gon' get our asses locked up. 'Cause you know if you swing, I'm swinging too."

Nate listened to me, but continued to give evil stares at both of the men. They looked scared as hell, and when they were out of our sights, that's when we started to pick up our pace. The Metrolink line was long as hell, but since they had so many of them running, we suspected it wouldn't take too long. We stood waiting, but Nate was still hyped.

"Ol' silly-ass motherfuckas," he ranted. "They need to keep that nigger shit in their homes, where most of them use that shit freely and around their kids. That's why this world so fucked up now, and this racism shit ain't never gon' be put to rest."

I agreed, but I didn't respond because it would only get him fired up. There were already plenty of police

officers hanging around, and being in the back of a police car tonight was not my ambition. That thought did
change when I spotted Poetry and her man coming my
way. She came right up to me and put her arms on my
shoulders. She leaned in, forcing her tongue inside of
my mouth. The taste of her lips were so sweet, I didn't
dare back away. Plus, I wanted to make her man mad,
and her boldness impressed me. I figured he was going
to start throwing blows, and a kiss that good may have
been worth a li'l jail time tonight. Poetry backed away,
leaving me stunned as hell.

"I figured you may have wanted to see more fireworks tonight and I hope you did. And if you still have
my number, as you say, then use it."

She removed her arms from my shoulders while
I stood there in a trance. I couldn't even think fast
enough, but when her boyfriend stepped forward, my
reflexes jumped. "This is my play brother, Trevon,"
Poetry said. "You thought you had me, but not quite."

Her play brother spoke and the two of them walked
away. Nate cocked his head back. "What was that all
about? Did you know her?"

"Somewhat," I said, thinking about what Poetry had
done. Hell yeah, I liked her, but was fighting everything
inside of me not to.

"Are you saying that you 'somewhat' let a gal kiss on
you who you barely knew? Shit, I wish I had a woman
step up to me and kiss me like that without knowin'
me. That would make any man feel good."

The lady in front of us joked with Nate about giving
him a kiss and their conversation led from one thing
to another. They exchanged phone numbers and all of
his attention had turned to her. That was a good thing,
because all of mine had turned to Poetry. I kept watching my back, hoping that she would walk up and put

another one on me. I didn't see her, but I was so sure she'd be visiting the laundromat soon. This time, I'd have my shit together.

# Chapter Five

## Man Down, Street Soldier Up

Still hadn't heard from Mama—yet. Another week had gone by, and I was really starting to get worried. When I called her house phone Raylo answered one time, saying that he hadn't heard from her either. After that one time, no one had been answering at all. I tried her cell phone when I got up this morning, only to hear that it had been disconnected. That prompted me to go over to her house, and as I stood in her bedroom, looking around, there appeared to be no sign of her. Raylo wasn't there, so I called his cell phone to see if he could tell me anything other than he didn't know where she was.

"Prince, you know how yo' damn mama is. She got mad at me that night and jetted. Threatened to never come back, but I didn't believe her. She'll be back, though. Just give her some time. It's all we can do right now, and even though I'm worried, I know she's somewhere safe."

"Somewhere safe like where, though? And did y'all just argue that night or did y'all have a fight? I talked to her the day before, and she sounded like everything was cool. She told me to bring her some cigarettes. I can't believe she's been gone since then."

"I can. We didn't have no fight, just an argument. She wanted me to go out and get her some cigarettes too, but I was tired that night. She started cursin' me out, and I told her to go fuck herself. Next thing I knew, she grabbed some of her shit and told me she would be back whenever."

I sighed, not knowing whether to believe Raylo. Mama was so good at doing shit like this, but something wasn't right this time. "Did she say anything about me? Or what to tell me if I called?"

"She was fussin' about you not bringin' her those cigarettes, and said if you called to tell you she'd get at you some other time. That's it, Prince. I don't know what else to tell you. As soon as she calls me, I'll let you know. Right now, I gotta get back to my game. I'm at the pool hall and the fellas are waitin' on me to take my shot."

Raylo hung up, but I wasn't satisfied with what he'd said. I went next door to the neighbors, asking if they'd seen Mama or if they'd heard anything. Mr. Brown was an old-ass man who lived next door. We didn't get along, nor did he and Mama. But he was nosy, and if anybody saw anything going wrong in the neighborhood, it would be him. He was watering his grass, or should I say mud, trying to get some grass to grow.

"Say, Mr. Brown," I said, stepping up to him. "I'm lookin' for my mama. Have you seen her around lately?"

"I . . . I think I saw her outside a few days ago. She was with another young lady. They got in a car and left."

"Had you seen the woman before? And what kind of car did they get into?"

Mr. Brown paused before answering. "I think it was one of those fast cars. Camaro or something like that."

I pointed to my car. "Like that one? Was it like that one?"

He scratched his head while looking at my car. "Yeah, that's it. It was that one, because I remember that thing hanging from the rearview mirror."

I thanked Mr. Brown, realizing that he didn't know what the fuck he was talking about. Mama didn't know anybody who drove a car like mine, and as far as I knew, none of her friends had a Camaro. I went to another neighbor's house. Her name was Pat, and even though she wasn't old as Mr. Brown was, her ass was on drugs. She was always outside, trying to see if she could hook up something. She was sitting on the porch smoking a cigarette when I walked up to her.

"Ay, Pat. Have you seen my mama around here lately?"

Pat blew smoke in the air, then crossed her skinny and frail legs. "Nah, I ain't seen her. But I've heard that big mouth of hers. She know she got a big-ass mouth and she be over there cussing yo' daddy's ass out."

"That nigga Raylo ain't my daddy. When's the last time you heard her yellin'?"

Pat sat for a moment, looking to be in thought. "Shit, Prince, I . . . I don't know. A week ago . . . maybe two. I haven't seen her in several days, though, and she often stops by to get some cigarettes from me. It's been a minute."

"You say a week or two, but have you seen her this week at all?"

"Naw. But if you see her before I do, please tell her to bring me my twenty dollars she owes me. Maybe that's why she ain't been comin' around. You know how people get when they owe you money. They ass get ghost." She laughed, and quite frankly, I agreed. I thanked Pat for the unhelpful info, and started to walk away.

"Prince," she said. I turned around, showing a bit of frustration on my face. "You lookin' good as hell.

Never knew you'd grow up and become such a sexy-ass young man, and if you ever want to get somethin' goin', let me know. I'm all yours. Tell Raylo to come see me, too. I need to get some of that, and he'll know what I'm talkin' about."

I wanted to tell her not to do me any favors, but all I did was smile and kept on walking. I didn't do crackheads, and even though Pat wasn't a bad-looking woman, those drugs had her looking as if she were fifty instead of thirty-five. I went back inside of Mama's house, hoping that she did leave with one of her friends a few days ago like Mr. Brown had said.

I stopped to use the bathroom, then went back into Mama's bedroom to look around. I pulled back her thick comforter on her bed and moved her pillows around. I opened her dresser drawers, trying to find any clues as to where she had gone. I even checked the phone, flipping through the numbers on the caller ID and writing down some of the numbers so I could call them later. I came up empty in her room, then, just for the hell of it, I checked mine. Like the last time, nothing was out of place and my room still looked the same. I closed the door and went into the kitchen, checking the drawers, cabinets, and closet. Nothing jumped out at me, so I plopped down at the kitchen table. I rubbed my tired eyes, then turned the cap on my head backward.

"Damn, Mama, where are you?" I said out loud. "Shit!"

Everything in my gut was saying that something was wrong. My eyes shifted around the room, and that's when I noticed a knife was missing from a knife set that had always sat on the counter. The only reason it jumped out at me was because Mama had pulled that knife out on me and Raylo plenty of times before. It was like her best friend, and she used it for protection whenever she got mad. Even when she was drunk and tripping, she'd always go for her knife and threaten to stab somebody with it. I got up from the table, looking everywhere that I could in the kitchen to find that knife. And nearly thirty minutes later, all I found, or should I say saw, was a dried bloodstain on her kitchen curtain. I held the curtain, trying to think if I remembered the stain being there. I hated to play detective, and even though I wanted to call the police to report her missing, I didn't want no shit. They'd start questioning me about other things and I wasn't about to set myself up like that. So, so far, I had the missing knife, the bloodstained curtain, and nothing else. That was, until I went into the living room and found something else. A handful of Mama's hair was by the couch. She hardly evercut her own hair, and if it was cut, she went to the beauty shop to have it done. I suspected it didn't fall out in a patch like the one I had in my hand, as this was odd. The way I looked at it, it was time for me to go confront Raylo man-to-man, because he obviously knew more than what he was saying.

I zoomed down Interstate 70, making my way to the pool hall that he frequented on Cass Avenue. I saw his Cadillac parked outside with several other raggedy-ass cars. I pulled the red double doors open and was hit with a song by Chuck Berry. The lighting was so dim I could barely see, but when I moved the hanging beads aside that draped beyond the arch-shaped doorway, that's when I saw Raylo and several of his partners playing pool. Raylo was sitting on a stool with a Hershey's Chocolate chick all over him. He was all smiles until he saw me coming his way. He couldn't care less that he'd been caught cheating on Mama, and for years he had made it known that he wasn't a one-woman man.

I stepped up to him, blocking his view from the pool table. "Questions," I said, folding my arms across my chest. "Why is my mama's knife in the kitchen missin'? Why is there blood on her kitchen curtains? And how in the hell did she lose this much hair?"

I held the patch of hair in my hand, just so he could see it. He removed the dangling toothpick from his mouth and sucked his teeth. Before saying anything to me, he turned to the woman next to him.

"Bitch, move. I need to get at this young punk about disrespectin' me and I don't want you to get hurt."

The woman gave him a kiss on the cheek before strolling away in a tight-ass dress that hugged nothing but rolls of fat. Her stench wasn't nothing to play with, either. How dare this sucker disrespect my mama with such trash? That made me even madder.

"Now, I'ma give you every opportunity to come at me again like you got some sense, young blood. If you don't, I will have to show you some of that shit I've been showin' yo' mama over the years. Maybe you will live and learn like she has; then again, maybe not. The choice is yours, and to quickly answer your question, nigga, I haven't seen yo' damn mama. I don't know nothin' about nothin' and that's all I'm goin' to say."

"Ray," one of his friends yelled. "You all right?"

"Ain't nothin' I can't handle, Fred. Y'all go'n ahead and finish the game."

I knew Raylo would say some shit to piss me off, and I also figured I would find myself in a fucked-up situation today. That didn't bother me one bit, only because, this time, I came prepared. "I ain't got no beef with you, Raylo. All I want to know is where in the fuck is my mama? You say you don't know, but I don't believe you. I need to know what's up, right now. I'm not goin' anywhere until I find out. If you want to throw another one of your weak-ass punches, feel free. Just know that I'll be back every damn day to question you about my mama until she shows up, or until I find her. So what's it gon' be?"

Raylo licked his crusty, thick lips, pressing them together. He stood and pulled up his pants, trying to intimidate me. He would always do that every time he got ready to put his hands on Mama. But when he looked down, he saw the tip of my Glock poking through my shirt. My hand was already on it.

"Let me repeat myself, before shit get out of hand and people start havin' regrets," he said. "As soon as I hear from yo' mama, I will call you. I can't explain no missin' knife, nor any bloodstains on curtains that have been hangin' for the past ten-plus years. Now, if you don't want to be staggerin' out of here with bullet holes riddled in you, I suggest you take this up with me later on yo' turf, not mine."

His eyes shifted behind him. I turned around, only to see about six of Raylo's partners with their guns aimed directly at me. Maybe this wasn't such a good idea, and taking out Raylo right now didn't seem like the sensible thing to do. I put my cap on straight, lowering it a bit to cover my eyes. "You'd better hope she shows up. Make some calls, drive around . . . do whatever you have to do to find her," I said. "Time will eventually run out for you, Raylo, and one day it's gon' come down to just you and me."

I turned, cutting my eyes at his partners who mean mugged me and showed no fear whatsoever behind my threats. All I could hear was Raylo laughing, and, as my back was turned, one of his partners came up from behind and put a gun to the back of my head. Yeah, I was scared, but didn't let it show as he pushed me outside and slung me to the ground. He was every bit of 250

pounds, and when it came to going to blows with niggas that big, I opted to go for the legs. I charged at him,
grabbing his legs and knocking him to the ground. His
gun flipped out of his hand and he started pounding
my back with his fist.

"Who, the, fuck, you, think, you, are," he said with
each pound. "Li'l nigga, I will kill yo' ass!"

I tightened my body, trying not to feel the hard blows
as we punched and tussled our way to the side of the
building. I was straight up out of breath fighting with
this dude, but I kept elbowing him in his midsection
and pushing him against the brick-wall building. I
had hoped to knock the breath out of him so I could
somehow get at my Glock, which was still tucked into
my jeans. But before I knew it, that fool had me in a
headlock.

"Now what?" he said, twisting my head tight, trying
his damnedest to break my neck. My ears felt as if they
were being ripped from my head, but I kept elbowing
the man as hard as I could in his stomach. I was trying
to reach my gun while bent over, but my hands were so
slippery that I couldn't quite get a grip. And as hard as
this fool was squeezing my head, I knew that I only had
a matter of seconds before he broke my damn neck.
Finally, I was able to remove my gun from my jeans,
and I wasted no time blasting that fool in his leg. Im-
mediately, he let go of me and staggered backward to
the building. His face was scrunched while he squeezed
his leg, attempting to stop the gushing blood.

I cocked the gun sideways, aiming it directly at his
head. "Now, see what yo' ass get? You had to be the
brave one, but look at your sorry ass now."

"We . . . we good," he said in a panic. "I . . . I wasn't
gon' hurt you, man. Just tryin' to teach you a lesson,
that's all."

I wanted to walk away; after all, I was doing my best to change my life around and stay away from all of the nonsense. But the whole thing with Raylo and Mama had my blood boiling over. For this nigga to inject himself in this was one big . . . huge mistake. I stepped up to him and pulled the back of his hair that was in a two-inch nappy afro. I rubbed the tip of my gun against his lips, watching them tremble.

"You wanted to teach me a lesson, huh?" I said.

He quickly nodded as the sheen of sweat from his forehead started to trickle down his face. "Yeah, man. That's all. No hard feelings, all right?"

I pushed the gun into his mouth, ordering him to suck on it. "Go ahead," I said. "Lick the hole and taste it real good. Then, I'ma teach you a lesson."

The man's eyes bugged as he rolled his tongue on my Glock and licked the hole. As his mouth widened just a tiny bit, I pulled the trigger, watching his blood splatter. "The lesson," I said, looking at his eyes that were now closed forever. "Don't fuck with me again."

I quickly jetted, feeling frustrated as ever and hating to go there. All kinds of thoughts were running through my head, but what I'd done to Raylo's partner was in the back of my mind. I was concentrating on Raylo. It really didn't make sense for him to do something to Mama, especially after all of these years. If he was going to kill her, he would have done so years ago. I had to believe that she was just mad at him and was taking it out on me too. Maybe she didn't want nobody to get in touch with her, and if that was the case, I was gon' get in her shit whenever I saw her again.

Before going upstairs to my apartment, I checked in at the laundromat to see how business was going. For a Sunday night, it was booming. It was only nine o'clock, and since I didn't feel like hanging around and listening to the women gossip, I decided to come back later. I made my way to the elevator, but instead of going upstairs, I stopped at Francine's door and knocked. It took a few minutes for her to answer, but when she did, she opened the door with a peach silk robe on. Her big breasts were damn near popping out, but she tried to tighten her robe to hide them.

"Can I come in?" I asked, already seeing the older man who was sitting in a kitchen chair behind her. I was known for popping up, and sometimes Francine would send me on my merry way, but sometimes she wouldn't. She invited me in, introducing me to one of her many sugar daddies, James. He tossed his head back, then looked at Francine.

"I guess this means I gotta go," he said.

"No hard feelings, James. Prince called about an hour ago and said he'd be here. I didn't know you were stopping by. Had I known, I would've told you not to come."

He stood, and without saying another word, Francine walked him to the door and he left. She closed the door, then picked up a cigarette that was already burning in an ashtray. "You gonna have to stop doing this shit, Prince. You be messing up my money, man, and James ain't one I want to keep dissin' like that."

"My bad. I just stopped to see what you was up to. If I had known you had company, I would've kept it movin'."

"That's what you always say," she said, blowing smoke into the air. She came over to me, as I was already sitting back on the couch. "What's the matter? I can see the stress written all over your face."

"No worries. Nothing that a good night's sleep can't cure."

Francine put the cigarette out in the ashtray. She stood in front of me, then untied her robe so I could see just a sliver of her thickness. She rubbed her finger in the crevice between her breasts, then sucked her finger into her mouth. "Sleep ain't the only thing that can cure the worried look in a man's eyes. You know what else can, but you need to start doing me some favors too."

I knew Francine was referring to me eating her pussy. I had never gone there with her, and she often complained. I wasn't feeling her like that, and even though the pussy was good, it was good for my dick, and not so much for my mouth. I rested my arms on top of the couch and leaned back. "Are you gon' start this shit with me again? I told you I don't get down like that, ma, didn't I?"

"That's what you say, but I know for a fact you be going down on Jenay. She ain't the kind of woman who would just settle for some dick, and with her, from what I hear, you gotta bring your A game. If you're bringing it with her, you need to be bringing it with me as well."

"I do bring my A game, but you need to know that I don't go down on nobody like that," I lied. Truth was, I had performed oral sex on Jenay, only because I liked having sex with her more than I did Francine. I just couldn't get to Jenay when I wanted to, because she was always busy with her other woman. I'd missed out the other night and hadn't heard from her since.

"I don't believe you, Prince, but next time, I'ma let James take care of me instead of you. This is some bullshit and you know it."

I shrugged, not mad at all. And once Francine unzipped my pants and saw how hard my dick was, she wasn't too mad either. She dropped to her knees, and I scooted closer so she could serve me well. As she got busy with her hands and mouth, I reached out my hands to massage her thick breasts. Those suckers had to be filled with a bunch of milk, and were soft as ever. Her Milk Duds–sized nipples were the only things hard, and the more I teased them, the harder they got. After a while, I reached down to dip my fingers inside of Francine's pussy. It was dripping wet. I could feel the creamy buildup already running down her legs. She was a nymphomaniac, but I loved every bit of it. That was, until she stopped sucking me and tried to maneuver us into a sixty-nine position on the couch.

"What did I tell you?" I asked with her pussy staring me right in the face.

"Come on, Prince. If I do you, what's the big deal with you doing me?"

I didn't want to mess up the mood by saying that the problem was she opened her legs to any nigga who desired to get in, but instead, I backed away from her. I stood up, stroking my own dick to keep it hard.

"Why you trippin'?" I asked in a polite manner. "You know I'ma make it good to you, and by the time I get finished, you won't be thinkin' about no oral sex."

"I doubt that, but you go ahead and do you."

I strapped on a condom, then got behind Francine as she was bent over on the couch. While pulling her hair back, I tore her insides up, causing her to tighten her fist and pound it on the couch.

"Fuuuuuk it, Prince! Daaaaamn this dick good as hell, nigga, fuck it!"

The more she talked, the faster I slammed into her. We started sweating and her ass had turned red from the beating I was putting on it. "Oh, shit, Prince! I'ma flood yo' ass with my juices. Here I come, damn it here I commmmmme!"

Francine's wetness was all over me. My semen had boiled over inside of the condom, and when I pulled out of Francine's pussy, my muscle went right into her mouth. She licked me clean while I lay back on the couch with my toes curled and my chest heaving.

"You know you got some good-ass stuff," I complimented while trying to catch my breath.

"So good that you don't want to suck it though, right?"

I didn't bother to respond. I could tell that Francine and I were about to catch some problems with this oral sex shit, so I got up to make a move. It would be awhile before I came back to her again.

"You getting ready to go already?" she asked while watching me put on my clothes.

"Yeah, I need to go check on the laundromat and clean up my apartment. I know you gotta work this week, so I won't come holla at you again until the weekend."

She put her hand on her hip. "You know that's lame as hell, Prince. You come over here whenever you feel like it, and trust me when I say that I don't mind. Just don't be catching no attitude with me about asking you for oral sex. Your sex be good too, but sometimes I be needing a little more action. It be all about you getting yours. You know that shit ain't fair."

"I agree, and you'll be the first to know when I decide to get down like that. Don't take it personal. The only reason I suggested chillin' until next week was to give you some time to get that oral satisfaction from someone else. I'm sure you will, and I don't want to keep on interruptin'."

"Whatever, Prince," she said, walking me to the door. "I'm cooking some lasagna tomorrow, so I'll at least be up there to bring you some of that."

"Sounds good to me. Holla."

Sex with Francine had cleared my mind for a little while, but my thoughts turned back to Mama. Just for the hell of it, I called the phone at the house, but got no answer. Called her cell phone; it was still disconnected. I hurried to lock up at laundromat, then went back upstairs to my apartment. Every time I called on God for Him to answer my prayer, He didn't seem to come through for me. At least, not in a way that I wanted Him to, but what did I have to lose? I closed my eyes, praying for Mama's safe return. I knew that if she didn't show up soon, all hell would break loose and I could feel some heat coming my way.

# Chapter Six

## Man On A Mission . . .

I was on a mission. And that mission was to find Mama. Everything inside of me said that something wasn't right, but I had not one piece to the puzzle. I had been stopping by her house two or three times a day, trying to see if she'd made her way home. I'd been following Raylo, but nothing he'd been doing was out of the ordinary. He was all about his women and hustling to make money. I didn't want him to catch wind of me following him around, but he was the only who I thought really knew where Mama was.

That was, until I went back to Mama's house and discovered a name, address, and phone number on a piece of paper that was tucked inside of a Greyhound Bus brochure in her dresser drawer. Several dates were written on the brochure, and it looked as if Mama may have checked out of here. I tucked the brochure in my pocket, then headed outside to my car. My cell phone was on the front seat, so I used it to dial the number that was on the piece of paper. I was surprised that someone actually answered.

"Monroe. Speak or forever hold your peace."

Monroe was the name on the paper, so I asked if his last name was Jackson, as that was on there too.

"You got me. Who is this?"

"Prince Perkins. I'm lookin' for my mama, Shante. Is there any chance that she may be with you?"

He cleared his throat. "Who is this again? I know Shante, but she ain't told me shit about havin' a son. Is this a joke or what?"

"No joke; and I don't care what she's told you. I'm tellin' you that I'm her son. If she's there with you, can I speak to her, please?"

"She ain't here right now. She went to the store, but when she gets back, I'll let her know you called."

"At the store, huh? How long has she been there with you and how long has she known you? I've never heard her mention your name before, and it seems odd that my mama would rush to Kansas City to hook up with you."

"Listen, youngster, Shante is a grown-ass woman who does not need the permission of her young adult son to do somethin'. Just like she didn't tell me about you, I guess she didn't tell you about me. We've hooked up plenty of times before and whenever I make way to St. Louis, I stop in to get at her. Now as I said before, I will let her know you called. If she wants to return your call, she will. If not, you'll just have to wait until she gets home. We're havin' a pretty good darn time, though, so I don't think that phone call will come your way anytime soon."

"One question: if my mama didn't tell you about me, then why would you refer to me as a youngster? I have your address on this piece of paper, so I'ma shoot your way to find out what's really up. Hopefully, my mama will be back from the store, and if not, we gon' have some problems."

I hung up, feeling as if this was a bunch of bullshit. I figured Mama wouldn't be stupid enough to play these kinds of games with me, and mad at Raylo or not, something didn't seem right. At this point, I had nothing to lose and all that mattered was the truth. A ride to

Kansas City would only take me three hours and when I punched Monroe's address into my GPS device, it showed that I could be there in exactly three hours and twenty-five minutes. With that, I slammed my door shut and headed to the gas station to fill up my tank. Still had to jet home to get a few things, but Kansas City here I come.

As I was pumping my gas, I could have sworn that I saw Raylo across the street with another person in the car. I squinted, trying to get a closer look, but the car quickly sped off. I stopped pumping the gas, just so I could get in my car and go follow them. I jetted down Lucas and Hunt, swerving in and out of traffic, trying to find the white Cadillac. I saw it stopped at a red light on Natural Bridge, but as soon as the light changed the car took off. The Cadillac was no match for my Camaro, but as I got closer to it I heard sirens. I looked in my rearview mirror, and sure enough, a police vehicle was behind me. I damn sure wanted to take off, but as I looked ahead of me, the Cadillac had gotten even farther away. I wondered what that was all about, but then again, I figured Raylo had been watching me as I'd been watching him. That made me even more suspicious about his ass, and I couldn't wait to find out what was up with him. First, I still had to make my way to Kansas City. I could only do so if the police officer who was approaching my car didn't have nothing on me. I lowered my window and looked up at him.

"Hello, Officer. Is there somethin' wrong?"

"Very wrong. You were speeding. Going as fast as you were, you put the lives of other motorists in danger. You're not wearing your seat belt and your license plates are due to expire tomorrow."

"Tomorrow ain't here yet, so I still have one more day. As for the speedin' thing, I was tryin' to keep up with the flow of traffic. The seat belt . . . My life, not yours."

The black officer stared at me from behind his dark shades and cocked his neck from side to side. "Let me see your license, registration, and proof of insurance. And make sure I can see your hands at all times."

I wanted to go off on his ass, but did my best to keep my cool. I gave him my license, registration, and a fake-ass insurance card that I had someone make up for me. No way in hell was I paying for no damn insurance, and if I ever crashed my car, I'd just buy me another one. If I hit somebody, they were just shit out of luck.

The officer walked back to his police vehicle, and I observed him through the rearview mirror. I wasn't sure if I had any warrants, or if I was wanted for any murders. All kinds of thoughts roamed in my head and I was so sure that I wouldn't make it to Kansas City to see about Mama. I tapped my sweaty fingers on the steering wheel, waiting and wondering what would ultimately happen. I could see the police officer on his walkie-talkie. He kept nodding his head, laughing, then looking at me. A few minutes later, another police car pulled up behind him. Now, anybody in their right mind knew that when two police cars came on the scene, some shit was about to go down. I wanted to take the fuck off, and as my heart rate increased, I sure as hell thought about doing so.

Instead, I waited. Both officers walked up to the car, and the one who had approached me before stepped up to the driver's side and reached for the handle.

"Jamal, step out of the car. Place your hands behind your head and make sure I can see them at all times."

I sighed, not knowing what the fuck was up. "Am I being arrested? If so, for what?"

"There's a warrant out for your arrest. You have un-paid tickets in Velda City and have failed to take care of them."

My faced scrunched. "What? Tickets? I ain't got no tickets, man."

By this time, the officer snatched me out of the car and read me my rights. I guess I could be thankful that I was only being arrested for tickets, but I seriously didn't remember getting any. Niggas were known for using other people's name, but I didn't have time to find out who was behind this. My goal was to pay the tickets, allow them to release me, and get on my way to Kansas City.

The officer handcuffed me behind my back, then asked me to take a seat along the curb. The shit was so damn embarrassing. Many cars drove by, people slowing down, just to see what the hell was going on. My head was lowered, and I shook it as I watched the officers go through my vehicle trying to find something that wasn't there. I guess it disappointed them when they couldn't find anything. Not even my Glock that I was lucky not to have in my possession. I had thought about taking it to Kansas City with me, but hadn't stopped by my apartment to get it just yet. This was a relief, as timing was everything. If he had stopped me an hour from now, I would definitely be going to jail for a long-ass time.

One of the officers stood me up. "Why haven't you paid your tickets?" he asked.

I knew better than to tell him that I didn't recall get-ting any tickets, so I went with the flow. "I didn't have no money to pay for them."

He reached in my fat pockets, pulling out a wad of money. "You may not have had money then to pay them, but you damn sure got money now. Where did you get all of this money from?"

I cocked my head back, starting to slowly but surely lose it. "I work. That's where I got it from."

"What kind of work do you do?"

"That ain't really yo' business. All you need to know is it's legal."

"I don't think that slanging dope is legal. Maybe in your head it is, and I better not catch you on my streets slanging shit. If I do, there will be some serious repercussions."

"I told you I wasn't slanging no dope. Every black man out here who got money ain't out here doin' illegal shit to get money. Many of us *do* work. A prime example would be you. You makin' money the legit way, ain't you? If you can do it, I can too. So, stop tryin' to find somethin' on me that ain't there. If you're goin' to lock me up for those tickets, do it. Let me pay my bail and let's be done with this."

The officer sucked his teeth, not liking my attitude at all. Thing was, as of right now, they had not a single thing on me but some unpaid tickets. He shoved me toward the police car, placing me in the back seat. The other officer called a towing service to tow my car, and all I could do was shake my head again. This shit was so goddamn ridiculous. It was all about making money and harassing people who had been subjected to this kind of foolishness for years. It took everything I had inside not to get my clown on with this officer, and for the most part, I remained calm, cool, and collected. That was until I got to the police station, and was told that my bail would be set at $1,000 and I had over $700 in tickets.

"Get the fuck out of here," I said, standing in front of the fat-ass sheriff's desk.

He looked at me with his crusty lips pursed. "Do you got it or not? If not, all you get is one phone call and it better be made to somebody who got some money or else you'll be here until the judge shows up on Tuesday morning."

I had about four grand rolled up in my pocket and when I inquired about it, the officer who arrested me claimed that there was only $2,000. He placed it on the counter in front of me. No doubt, my stack had become smaller.

"Y'all motherfuckas be killin' me. I know how much money I had and it damn sure wasn't no two grand," I said.

He got up in my face, mean mugging me and spitting in it. "What you trying to say? Fool, I didn't take a dime of your money, so get your lies together. Punk!"

I took deep breaths, knowing that this could escalate into something I didn't want it to. I definitely didn't have time to be locked up in no jail cell for several days, so I changed my tune. "You're right," I said, with my hands still cuffed behind my back. "Now I remember. I did only have two grand. That's enough to take care of my bail and for the tickets. Go ahead and process me so I can be released. And, uh, sorry for the mishap . . . I was trippin'."

Both the sheriff and the officer looked at each other and smirked. I was sure they would be somewhere eating dinner tonight or making it rain up in a strip joint with my money, but what the hell? This was a no-win situation and I knew that from the moment he pulled me over.

"Take him back to a cell until we're done processing him," the sheriff said to the officer.

He reached for my arm, escorting me to a nearby holding cell that had a small, flat bed in the corner. The cell smelled like piss, and instead of sitting on the bed, I sat on the dirty concrete floor.

"Don't get too comfortable." The officer laughed as he locked the cell.

"I assure you I won't," I snapped. "Just hurry it the fuck up."

He snickered, then walked away.

I hated the police—let me repeat . . . hated them. There was nothing positive that I had ever seen about them and all they did was harass the black man. I figured that was part of their training session, and many of the motherfuckas around here did their jobs well. Nearly two hours later, the officer came back to my cell, telling me I was clear to go. He gave me some papers to sign, then handed me the $300 that was left of my money.

"Next time," he said, handing me a business card. The card was from the tow yard that had my car. "Slow down and take care of your tickets. Think about a better career than selling drugs and watch your tongue, as it's liable to get you hurt and in more trouble."

I headed toward the door, completely ignoring the officer. All I did was salute on my way out, and I had to wait for a taxi to come get me so I could go to the tow yard and pick up my car.

The taxi took about thirty minutes to get there, and another thirty minutes to get to the tow yard. The man behind the counter at the tow yard had an attitude, too, and this bullshit was seriously driving me crazy. I had to drop $150 just to get my car back. Like I said . . . anything to rip off a black man and keep him down by taking his money. The entire system was fucked up and was designed so that niggas like me wouldn't get ahead.

Finally, my car was released to me and I headed home to get more money and my Glock. On the way out, I was stopped by Francine, who wanted to borrow some money. With all the pussy she was giving away, it was odd that she was broke.

"I'll give it back to you in a couple of weeks, Prince. You know I'm good for it."

"Sorry, ma, I ain't got it. Not right now."

She put her hands on her hips. "Come on, Prince. You know you got it. It ain't that often when I ask you for something. And as much as I give to you, money shouldn't be no issue with us."

I was starting to dislike Francine more and more by the day. Some chicks always wanted payment for some pussy and Francine acted as if I owed her something. "What did I say?" I responded, while heading toward the door to the building. "Again, I don't have any money to loan."

"Twenty dollars!" she shouted. "You can't give me twenty damn dollars? Okay, I'm good. The next time you want something from me, I'ma tell you no too."

I shrugged, not really caring that Francine would hold back on having sex with me. It wasn't like I couldn't get it anywhere else, and quite frankly, sex was the last thing on my mind. Getting to Kansas City was the priority and I was sure Mama had made it back from the store by now.

Finally, I was on the road, frowning at times from my thoughts, and then rapping to the lyrics that were coming through my speakers. I was almost in Kansas City, and according to the GPS tracking device, I would reach my destination within forty-five minutes.

For some reason, I started to think that Mama was playing a game with me. Was she that mad because I hadn't brought those items to her when she wanted them? Then again, if getting away from Raylo was her reason for disappearing, I was all for it. It was about damn time, and all I needed to do was hear her say so.

I needed to see her, just to make sure everything was okay. After that, I didn't give a damn who she was with. As long as she wasn't with another abusive man, I was cool.

I parked in front of a small brick house that looked to be dead smack in the hood. Niggas were lurking around, watching me from afar. I was skeptical about getting out of my car, but had to get out to see what was up. I noticed trash was piled up on the side of the house and debris from the trash was on the grass. The porch was leaning and the screen door with holes in it wasn't even necessary. I couldn't believe that Mama would come all this way to spend time with a broke-ass fool. Even though Raylo wasn't working a nine-to-five, he still managed to keep money in his pockets. It was obvious, by the look of this place, this brotha didn't have much.

I opened the screen door, knocking several times before I heard the volume from the music inside go down.

"Who is it?" the man inside shouted.

"Prince!"

"Who!"

"Shante's son! Is she here?"

There was silence. I waited for a minute or two, then banged on the door again. "Ay, what's up? Is my mama here or not? I need to get at her about somethin'."

No answer. I didn't know what kind of games this damn fool was playing, but whatever it was, I wasn't in the mood for it. I banged again, shaking the door and causing the windows to vibrate. Finally, the man pulled on the door, looking at me with red, fiery eyes. The aroma of marijuana filled my nostrils, along with the funk that was seeping outside from the inside of his house.

The man's wrinkly face twisted. "I told you yo' mama wasn't here, didn't I?"

"Where is she then? You said she went to the store and would be right back."

"Well, she ain't made it back yet. Now get the fuck off my porch with all this attitude and go home."

I took a few steps back, knowing damn well that this was not going to be a wasted trip for me. Reaching in my pocket, I touched the tip of my Glock, thinking about when to make my move. "Monroe, you have only a few minutes to tell me where my mama is. If not, this shit about to get ugly. Do you know where my mama is, or is this some kind of game yo' ass playin' with me?"

Monroe looked me over with his beady eyes and sucked his teeth. I could tell he was thinking of a lie, but I damn sure wanted to hear it. Before I knew it, though, he stepped back and tried to slam the door in my face. That angered me, and before he could close the door, I pushed on it. My finger got slammed in the crack, and burned as I felt much pain.

"Shit," I yelled, as the door did not close. I had already reached for my gun with my other hand, and after Monroe saw it, he rushed away from the door. My first instinct was to shoot, but what good would that have done if I needed some answers?

Before I knew it, Monroe was standing in the long hallway with his gun aimed at me at the front door.

My gun was aimed at him.

"I don't want to go out like this with you, bro," he said. "But you can't be comin' up in here throwin' no tantrums 'cause you can't find yo' mama. I will kill yo' ass, then call the police and claim you were an intruder. The choice is yours. Either you leave now, or you leave this motherfucker in a body bag."

"I will leave, once you tell me what's up with my mama. That's all I want to know, man, and we can squash this shit right here and right now. Ain't nobody got to die over no bullshit like this. If your mama was missin', you'd want to know where the fuck she was too, right?"

Monroe stood silent for a while, then spoke up again. "I don't know where she is. She came here for a day or two and left. Hasn't called me since."

"What did she come here for? And why you lie to me about her still being here then?"

"'Cause I don't tell strangers everything I know. I didn't know who the fuck you were calling. She came here to have a good time with me. I told you we sometimes hook up, didn't I?"

I lowered my gun, feeling a bit more at ease and wanting him to feel the same. "Well, why haven't I ever heard her mention your name before? It's kind of odd that this is the first time I ever heard of you. Your name, number, and address just popped up on a piece of paper today."

Monroe lowered his gun and took a few steps forward. He sat on the couch and picked up a blunt that was in the ashtray. "I don't know why yo' mama never mentioned me. I've been around for a long time. You'd have to talk to her about that but, unfortunately, I don't know where she is right now. She came here upset about somethin', but didn't want to tell me what was wrong. We hung out, had sex, drank a li'l . . . and then she went on her way."

I let out a deep sigh, not feeling a word this brotha was saying. He was trying too hard to convince me that Mama was here, but he had no proof. "When she came, what was she drivin'? I suspect she didn't come all this way on foot."

He took a few hits from the joint, then passed it to me. Feeling as if I needed something, I took the joint from his hand and took a couple of hits from it too. I moved back to the chair behind me, waiting for Monroe to answer.

"She came here in a taxi. When we got done, she called one to come pick her up. Said she'd call me once she got back home, but that hasn't happened yet."

I sat, smoking up the blunt and realizing that I had wasted my time. "Monroe, my mama just colored her hair. Tell me somethin'. What color is it?"

He shrugged, then twisted his lips to the side. "Shit . . . I'on know. I believe it was dark brown or something like that. She looked good though. Real good."

"Did you see how short she'd cut her hair?"

He crossed his leg and looked down at the floor. "Yeah, yeah, I noticed that. Got one of those cuts those young gals be wearing."

I chuckled and took one last hit from the joint. I then stood to give it to him so he could finish it off. He took it, and inhaled to calm his rattled nerves.

"By any chance, did you see any bruises on her," I asked. "I mean, just in case she didn't tell you, she and Raylo argue a lot. The day before she disappeared, they got into an argument. I think he beat her up real bad, and the last time I saw her, her face was swollen. Her cattish gray eyes were like fire, and she didn't even look like my mama anymore."

Monroe dropped his head and shook it. "Yep, I told her about messin' around with that nigga. Her face must have healed, but those pretty gray eyes she got always melts my heart. I sholl be glad when she leave that fool alone. I told her she could come stay here with me, if she wanted to."

I sat back in the chair, touching the minimal hair on my chin. My Glock was still by my side, and as Monroe picked up the joint to take his last long hit, I lifted my gun and fired off two shots from a distance. The bullets pierced the air, landing right into the center of his chest. He didn't even know what had hit him, and as his eyes shot open, they shortly thereafter closed. His hand trembled and wiggled on top of his chest and I stood glaring at him, waiting and watching as he took his last breath.

"Gray eyes, short hair my ass," I said, tucking the gun inside of my pants. Obviously, this fool had never met or seen Mama before. He had been trying to play me for a fool, and too bad I was unable to pump more information from him about how his name, number, and address just somehow mysteriously appeared on Mama's dresser. I truly believed that Raylo was behind all of this shit, and he'd soon have to answer to me about what the fuck was really going on.

When I left Monroe's house, more niggas were standing around, trying to see what was up with me. I hated to be stared down and the looks on their faces implied that they wanted to say something. I didn't want to get into no shootout with the brothas, so I held my mouth shut and kept it moving. Got in the car and cautiously drove away. Thoughts about those sly-ass police officers were in my head, and I thought about the man back there who I had just put to rest. More than anything, I wondered . . . where in the fuck was my mama!

# Chapter Seven

### Deal, Or No Deal . . .

On Wednesday morning, I got a visit from Raylo that was completely unexpected. I was at the liquor store, working for Nate, who had taken the day off. While I was in thought about my decision not to pursue Poetry who, by the way, I hadn't heard from since Fair St. Louis, Raylo knocked on the door. I was just about ready to open up and there he was.

"I got somethin' real important that I need to get at you about," he said in a whisper. "And, when I tell you some of my partners want you dealt with, I mean it. They want me to lay you out right now, but you like my son, and we ain't got time to be goin' after each other. Besides, Kenny should have minded his own damn business that day at the pool hall. My opinion . . . he got what he deserved, and this other shit I need to get at you about is way more important."

I let Raylo inside, but locked the door after him. I was never one to admit what I'd done, so I played dumb. "Don't know what you're talking about with Kenny, but what's so important?" I asked. "Did you find out where Mama is?"

"So . . . somethin' like that," he said. "But what I found out ain't good news."

My heart dropped to my already tightened stomach. I knew Raylo hadn't come here to tell me something bad had happened to Mama. He seemed to be stalling, and that caused aggravation to show all over my face. "Go ahead and spill it. What do you know?"

"I got a call early this mornin' from somebody who told me yo' mama was with him. Said he wanted to talk to you about some shit you did to his brother, and that he wasn't goin' to let yo' mama go until you came to see him. I told him that I wasn't about to give him yo' info, but I would take his number and have you get at him. I also told him that if he did or had done anything to hurt Shante, that I would find out who he was and kill 'im. I suspect this has somethin' to do with that mess you got yourself into with those so-called friends of yours. And I'll repeat what I said to him, and say it to you. If anything happens to Shante because of this, somebody gon' get hurt. You'd better hope it won't be you, so do whatever you gots to do to fix this. Get back with me later on to let me know the deal."

Raylo gave me the nigga's number who called him this morning. I waited until Raylo had pulled off until I called to see what was up. When I did, the person who answered didn't say anything.

"Ay, this Prince. Somebody lookin' for me?"

"Yep. And, if you want to see yo' mama again, nigga, you need to make a move to come see me. Soon."

"Who is this? And, if you got my mama, let me speak to her."

"I call the shots, not you. You need not worry about who I am. All you need to know is we need to make some shit right. Take down my address and meet me within the hour. If you're late, I'll assume that you don't want to see your mama again and I'll also pretend as if this conversation never happened."

"What's the address?"

He gave it to me and hung up before I could ask any more questions. I was so in a rush to find out what was going on that I didn't have time to open the liquor store. I jumped into my Camaro, making sure my Glock was by my side, then took off down Union Boulevard to Lindell. I arrived at my destination several minutes later, noticing that the address I had written on the paper was a high-rise loft near the Central West End. I had to key in the code that somebody gave me, and when I did, I was buzzed to come in. I took the elevator to the fourteenth floor, then looked down the long hallway for door number 1432. When I found it, I knocked and stood for a moment with my hands in my pockets. I wasn't nervous at all, because I felt if anybody wanted to do away with me, it wouldn't be done in no upscale place like this. My only concern was finding out where Mama was.

Without asking who I was, a 300-pound nigga resembling Rick Ross opened the door. His shirt was open and his belly was hanging down low. Beard looked as if it hadn't been shaved in decades, but when I entered the loft, it was off the chain. Everything was black, including the fuzzy black rug that covered a portion of the shiny hardwood flooring. Tall black columns surrounded the spacious living room and the view from the huge picture window was breathtaking.

"Take a seat on the couch," the man said. "I'll be with you in a minute."

I took a seat on the black leather sectional that filled most of the room. Contemporary art covered the walls and a crystal light hung from the high, vaulted ceiling. The kitchen to my left had all stainless-steel appliances and it was spotless. A blond white chick with a robe on came from one of the rooms. She poured herself a glass of wine, then smiled at me.

"Would you like some?" she asked.

"No. Do you know where what's-his-face is? If you would go tell him that I have somewhere else I need to be, I'd appreciate it."

Just then, the dude who answered the door came back into the room. All he'd done was change his shirt to another one that was left open, showing his fat gut.

"Peaches, I need privacy," he said to the woman. She carried her drink into another room and closed the door. The man came over to the couch, causing it to sink as he sat across from me.

"Prince Perkins," he said with a sly-ass smirk on his face. "I can't believe I've come face-to-face with the nigga who murdered my li'l brother. I should be jumpin' over that table and beatin' yo' ass, but I'm not gon' do that unless you prompt me to. Besides, I have a better solution for this li'l problem you and I seem to have."

I played dumb. Again, the last thing I ever did was admit to murdering anyone; whether it was justified or not, my lips were sealed. "Don't know what you're talkin' about. The only problem that we seem to have is the one you may catch if you don't tell me where my mother is."

The man laughed and slapped his leg. "Boy, you are a tough li'l motherfucka, ain't you? You got balls and I sure as hell could have used you on my team. But I can't make friends with someone who did what you did. You slaughtered my brother in that bathroom that day, and even though he was guilty of killin' your girl-friend, he didn't deserve to die like that. My mama was distraught, and whenever you upset my mama, well, I have to upset yours—if you know what I mean."

I felt myself about to lose it, but was doing my best to remain calm. "This chitchat is real nice but, please, tell me why I'm here. I have business to tend to and, if you have news about my mama, you need to say somethin'."

"Your mother is fine. She's missin' you though, so the quicker you cooperate, the better off we all will be. She's safe, for now, but she won't be unless you chalk up one hundred fifty Gs. That will help minimize my pain and sufferin', and maybe I can go buy somethin' nice for my mother to help calm her nerves. She's been messed up ever since and money always has a way of changin' people."

"I don't have that much money, and what would make you think that a youngster like me got that kind of money floatin' around? It would take me forever to come up with somethin' like that, but if you let me speak to my mother, and she tells me that she's okay, then maybe—"

"Maybe my ass, Prince. You got it. I know you got some money stashed away and you know it too. See, a little birdie told me that you did some mad shit back in the day. I heard you blew your own daddy's fuckin' brains out, then took some of his money. That's some cold shit, man, and word on the street is you are not the li'l nigga to fuck with. Then, how you got at my brother and his friends . . . That was some straight Street Soldier shit. Don't you know there are consequences for doin' shit like that? You need to pay up and let some of your problems go away. One hundred and fifty thou is chump change for what you've done, and at least I'm not tryin' to break you."

"For the last time, I don't have that kind of money. Never have, never will. Now, you need to tell me where I can find my mama. If not, your mother gon' be down two sons, instead of one. And that ain't no threat, that's a promise."

I stood up, feeling as if this conversation was over. I wasn't going to be tricked into giving this nigga no money, and he wasn't even willing to let me speak to Mama. This was a waste of my time and it seemed as if this fool needed me more than I needed him. I made my way to the door, but was stopped when I heard Mama's voice on a tape recorder. "Prince gon' get you, nigga! Let me go!" she shouted. The man turned off the recorder, then walked toward me.

"That's all you gon' get for now," he said. "You think about what I said. You got five days to come up with my money. If you don't, your mother will be sharing space with my brother real soon."

He opened the door and I walked out. I was fuming inside, and so unsure about what to do. The tape recorder with Mama's voice on it wasn't enough to let me know she was still alive. I needed to hear from her, now! My mind was going a mile a minute. Yes, I had the money, but giving away one hundred and fifty Gs would break me. I would surely have to live off of the money from the liquor store and the laundromat, but that money wasn't enough to make me comfortable. I knew that getting Mama back was worth every single penny, but this nigga seemed as if he had it out for me. He couldn't be trusted, and no matter how hard I looked at this situation, it didn't seem like it was going to turn out pretty.

I zoomed down the street, dialing Raylo's number at the same time.

"Where you at?" I asked.

"At yo' mama's house. Did you call to see what was up with ol' boy or what?"

"Yeah, I did. I'm on my way to holla at you about some things."

"Sure," was all Raylo said, and hung up.

I hated Raylo, but I needed his help on this one. Maybe I was wrong about him being involved in Mama's disappearance, and there was no way for me to deal with this situation alone.

The front door was open. Raylo was sitting at the kitchen table waiting for me when I arrived. I leaned against the counter and folded my arms.

"Here's the deal," I said. "One of the niggas who I shot up at the lounge that day had a brotha. He was the one who reached out to me, saying that he kidnapped Mama. He wants a hundred and fifty Gs and he'll let her go. I don't know if I can trust him, and I really don't know if he has Mama because he didn't let me speak to her. All he did was play a recorder where I heard her voice. I need your help, because I don't know if this fool being truthful with me."

Raylo stared at me, then sucked his teeth. "You mean to tell me that you got Shante caught up in your bullshit, and now you're here askin' me for help! If you have the motherfuckin' money, yo' ass betta pay up so she can get her ass back here where she belongs! Do you not think she is worth it, or do you have another plan to go shoot up some more niggas and make more trouble for yourself? If so, you can count me out. My shoot-'em-up days are over. I only kill niggas who fuck with me, not ones who want to make you pay for what you did. I don't know what you want—"

"What I want is for you to shut the fuck up and listen. Okay, so I knew some shit was gon' eventually swing my way, but Mama ain't have nothin' to do with this. If you love her so much, then you'll put all that other bullshit aside and help me figure this out. I mean, what would you do? I have some of the money, but not all of it right now. If I deplete all of my funds, I may have more, but that's gon' leave me high and dry. Then, the biggest thing is I haven't talked to Mama. This fool could be settin' me up. How do I know Mama is still alive when haven't spoken to her?"

Raylo put his hands behind his head, giving me a stern look. "You do need to speak to her before you up anything. Give me that nigga's phone number and address. I'll do some investigations to see what I can come up with. Do not give him one red cent until I let you know what I find out. I may even pay him a visit myself, and I'll find out, for sure, if he has Shante."

"He says I got five days to bring him the money. After that, I don't know what he's goin' to do."

"Just calm down and let me handle this. Don't do nothin' until I tell you to. I'll call you later on today, and we'll go from there."

I stepped forward, slamming my hand against Raylo's and thanking him. "I know we've had some beef between us lately, but you need to know that I love yo' mama and I miss her too. I'm in this damn house goin' crazy, and the sooner she comes back to us, the better."

"I agree," I said, reaching into my pocket. I gave Raylo $500, only because I felt bad for accusing him of doing something to Mama, and for being stingy with my money. "That's all I have on me. And you know it will put a dent in my pockets if I have to come up with this money, so work with me, all right?"

Raylo looked at the money, then gave it back to me. "Don't worry about it right now. Let's see what we gotta do to get yo' mama back here, then we'll go from there. Go cool out and I'll get at you soon."

I nodded and left, hoping that Raylo could help me with this. Got in my car, and as soon as I got to the laundromat, I saw Poetry's car parked out front. This chick's timing was always off, and yet again, hooking up with her was the last thing on my mind right now. I walked inside, looking straight ahead and doing my best to ignore her. That in no way worked for her. As soon as I stopped to get a soda, she came over to the machine and stood next to me.

"Morning, handsome," she said, showing her snow-white teeth. "I thought you were goin' to call me. And have you given any consideration to offering me a job yet? I sure could use one."

"I can't call you if I don't have your number. As for the job, haven't given it much thought at all. But, uh, I need to go across the street to open my store. I'll check back with you later."

Surprised by my attitude, Poetry backed up and moved out of my way. I opened the door to my office, got another set of keys from my drawer, and left. I hurried across the street to open the liquor store for business.

All throughout the day, I waited on customers, trying my best to clear my thoughts. I kept picturing Mama somewhere tied up and being beaten. I saw her pleading for someone to spare her life, then I visualized her dead. I wanted to go kill somebody, but I was so unsure how all of this was going to pan out. Yet again I felt at fault for bringing hurt to the ones I loved and cared about the most. Now I was glad that Nadine's mother had left with my son. He didn't need to be around me and my mess. Eventually, he'd wind up paying for my mistakes. No matter where he was, he was damn sure better off than being with me.

"Seven dollars," I said to the woman on the other side of the window who had just purchased some lottery tickets.

She put her money on the revolving tray and I gave her her tickets. Some kids were in line behind her, and right behind them was Poetry. The kids wanted some pickles, soda, and a whole lot of candy. I rang up their items, and after they paid, I put the items in the tray. When Poetry stepped up to the window, she was not smiling. She placed a piece of paper on the tray, and when I swung it around, her phone number was written on it.

"Now you have my number, again, and I hope you plan to use it," she said. "Are you? And let me know about the job thingy."

I shrugged, looking at the growing line of customers behind her. "I don't know if I'm goin' to use your number yet. We'll see."

"We'll see? I need a yes or no. I don't—"

I quickly cut her off and nudged my head toward the door, buzzing it. "Come inside. I need to tackle my customers behind you, if you don't mind."

Poetry walked over to the door and opened it. I told her to have a seat. "What can I get you?" I asked the old woman who stood at the window.

"Do you have any Spam?"

"No, ma'am. But I do have some packs of bologna."

"Well, give me a pack with a loaf of bread."

I got the bologna and bread for the woman and rang up her items. Poetry sat quiet until I got a break after waiting on the last customer in line.

"So, what's up with you, Prince? Am I wasting my time with you or what?"

I didn't want Poetry to think that she was wasting her time, but her timing was off. I had too much shit going on right now, and the last thing I needed was a chick with demands. I didn't know how to say that to her without her feeling as if I was trying to be a pain. "This . . . this thing with you and me ain't good for me right now. I got some shit goin' on that I need to take care of, and it ain't nothin' against you. I think you fine and sexy as hell. Any other time I would get with you in a heartbeat, but not right now. Can't do it."

"Are you involved with somebody? I see you working all the time, Prince, and I'm trying to offer my help. Besides that, I ain't never seen a chick by your side. What's up with that? If you say the timing ain't right, tell me why."

I really didn't want to get into details, and was saved by the bell when Jenay walked in looking scrumptious as ever. The short skirt she had on showed all thighs and her breasts peeked through a V-neck halter that she wore. She came up to the window smiling. I couldn't help that I was all smiles too.

"What can I get you?" I asked.

Her pretty, round, seductive eyes stared at me through the glass, and not once did she take her eyes off me to look at Poetry. "Let's see," she said, finally shifting her eyes to the goods behind me, then back at me. "Okay, now I see what I want," she teased in a soft and seductive tone. "What happened to you the other night? I was surprised that you didn't show up. We had so much fun without you."

"Somethin' came up. Too bad I missed out, but maybe next time."

"Maybe so. Give me a Diet Pepsi, a stick of Juicy Fruit gum, and two Powerball tickets. Maybe I'll get lucky tonight."

"I hope so," I said, trying not to show my enthusiasm because Poetry was watching my every move. See, this was the kind of mess that I didn't want to have to answer to. I was so sure that Poetry would have something to say, and as soon as Jenay waved good-bye, and blew me a kiss on her way out the door, Poetry got it in.

"At least I now know why you be acting all funny and shit. She got you wrapped around her finger. How old is Miss Cougar?"

"That ain't the reason. Jenay is not my woman. She's my neighbor."

"I couldn't tell she wasn't your woman. Your face been flat all day, and as soon as she walked through the door, you would have thought Jesus stepped up in here or something. I guess I need to hike my skirt up a little higher, weave my hair all down my back, and get some breast implants in order for you to notice me."

"You ain't got to do all that, and I have noticed, all right? Just chill out for a while, and let what's gon' happen, happen. I got your number and I won't throw it in the trash. I'll call you as soon as I can and we can talk about us, as well as that job. You have my word that I will call. Soon."

"I hope you keep your word. I'm going to get out of your hair and go holla at my friend across the street. You be good and don't go getting yourself in no trouble, if you know what I mean."

Poetry left. All I did was smile, knowing that she was referring to Jenay. And after seeing her, I did want to get myself into some trouble. Jenay knew how to relax me and put my mind, body, and soul at ease. There was something about being with older women that made me feel that way. Just like the attraction I had for Patrice, I felt the same way about Jenay. Needing a quickie, and craving some relaxation, I put the OUT TO LUNCH sign on the door and headed upstairs. Jenay's apartment was directly across the hall from mine, so I lightly knocked on her door. She opened it, wearing a fishnet black shirt that revealed her bare breasts underneath and black thong that rested between her juicy pussy lips.

"I knew you would come, but not this soon," she said. "I was getting ready to take a shower and wash my hair. Give me about thirty minutes and I'll be ready for you then."

My dick had already shot up from looking at her. I eased one of my arms around her waist, bringing her body close to mine so she could feel my hardness. She leaned in for a kiss, and as our tongues slow danced, I moved my hand down to get a squeeze of her fat ass. I was about to explode.

Jenay moved her head back, halting our kiss. "Twenty minutes," she said. "I'll hurry."

I didn't want to let her go, until I heard talking and turned my head. Poetry was walking down the hall with a chick whose apartment was three doors down from mine. Both of them stopped in their tracks to look at Jenay being tightly held in my arms. She lifted her finger, turning my head to face her.

"Fifteen minutes. Now let me go shower and don't keep me waiting."

When she leaned in for another kiss, I couldn't back away. I did make it short, though, and backed away as she closed the door. I looked down the hall as Poetry turned her head, waiting for her friend to unlock the door. Afterward, they both went inside and I went into my apartment as well. Don't know why I felt bad that Poetry had seen me with Jenay, and why I even cared. I brushed it off, anxiously waiting for the fifteen minutes to go by. Wanting to check in to see if Raylo had any new news, I called his cell phone, only to get voice mail.

"Ay, holla back soon. I know it hasn't been long since we talked, but you know I'm anxious for you to find out what you can. The clock is still tickin'."

As soon as I hung up, there was a knock at my door. I pretty much knew who it was, so I skimmed my studio apartment, making sure the open space wasn't too junky. A few dishes were in the sink, the kitchen table had some crossword puzzle books on it, and some of my video games were on the floor. I quickly picked them up, then hurried to turn my sofa sleeper back into a couch. The plug-in Glade air freshener was working magic, so I was good with the way my apartment smelled. I opened the door, barely able to look Poetry in her eyes. Basically, I had just told her that I didn't have time for women, and minutes later, there I was with my arm wrapped around one and kissing her. I didn't feel as if I had any explaining to do, but Poetry didn't see it that way.

"I feel like a complete fool," she said, walking inside while I dropped back on the couch and put my hands behind my head. "I don't know what made me pursue you like I did, and if you had a woman, all you had to do was say so. You didn't have to deny it, Prince. Why let me continue to make a fool of myself, knowing that your resisting had everything to do with that tramp across the hall?"

"It doesn't have nothin' at all to do with Jenay. I told you that I'm not involved in a relationship with no one. Truthfully, all we do is have sex every now and then, and it ain't really no big deal. Why you sweatin' me like you're my woman or somethin'? I'm confused by all of this and I barely know you."

"I didn't come here to get in your shit about who you're with. All I'm saying is you should have told me to back the fuck off."

"I have been tellin' you that, but you ain't hearin' me. I told you all I was interested in was sex and nothin' else. That's all Jenay or any other chick that I'm down with will get. I suspected that you wanted much more than that, but if you don't, hey, take a number."

"Why take a number when I'm already here?" Poetry said, pulling her stretch dress over her head. She dropped it on the floor while standing in her matching turquoise lace bra and boy shorts. "All you men ever think about is sex. Don't no damn body know shit about love and relationships anymore! So come on and get some, Prince. I'll give it to you and you can have all the sex you want."

Poetry was being sarcastic, but she looked mad sexy in her skin. She had taken off her bra and when she lowered her boy shorts to her ankles, my dick was swollen. Those thoughts of Jenay went right out the window, and Poetry's shaved pretty pussy made me want to dive into it face first. But as much as I said it was all about sex, I didn't want to get down with her like that. There was something about her that I genuinely liked, but didn't have time to pursue.

"Don't sit there staring at me," she said. "Take off your clothes and let's break the damn ice. I'm sure I'll get you to call me after I suck your dick; then again, maybe not. We gotta start somewhere, and if it starts with us fucking, then let's."

I couldn't say nothing, and when Poetry came closer, I got up from the couch. I pulled the sheet off of it, trying to cover her naked body. She snatched the sheet away.

"What you doing?" she asked. "Ain't this what you want? You said you wanted sex, so why you trippin' and running like a scared chicken when I'm trying to give it to you?"

"'Cause I don't want just sex from you," I said with a sigh. "One day I'ma tell you all that's goin' on with me, but not right now. You gotta be patient and stop tryin' to rush this. I do like you, a lot, but give me—"

My cell phone rang, interrupting our conversation. As soon as I answered, a knock was also at the door. "What's up?" I said, seeing Raylo's number on the caller ID.

"McDonald's. Kingshighway and Natural Bridge. In thirty minutes, be there."

He hung up and so did I.

"Listen, I gotta go," I said, looking at Poetry. When I opened the door, she covered herself with the sheet. Jenay was at the door, and she could see Poetry standing behind me.

"Sorry, but I need to go make a run," I said to Jenay. "I'll stop by later."

"Don't forget," was all she said, and went back to her apartment.

I turned to Poetry, trying to speed things along so I could go. "I do not want to hurt your feelings, but I need for you to put your clothes back on so I can go. Somethin' urgent came up, and if you give me a chance, I'll explain it to you later."

Poetry slipped her dress over her head, put her bra and boy shorts in her purse, and looked at me while at the door. "You told her you'll stop by later, and you said you'd explain it to me later. I wonder which one of us you'll keep your word to."

I didn't respond. My mind was elsewhere right now, and I hoped Raylo had some good news for me.

# Chapter Eight

## Ladies and Gentlemen, Miss Poetry Wright . . .

As usual, McDonald's on Kingshighway and Natural Bridge was the hangout. I spotted Raylo in the far corner, eating some fries and licking the salt from his fingers. I hurried to join him at the table.

"So, what's the word?" I asked.

"Word is you got yourself and yo' mama in some deep, deep trouble. I found out who that fool was who you met today and his name is Geronimo. They call him G for short and his brother was the one who you killed at the lounge that day. One of my partners who know G says that he got some connections with some important people in St. Louis, includin' the chief of police. Don't know if he's tryin' to set you up, but G is money hungry. Him and his brother really didn't get along, so in a sense, you really did do him a favor. I don't think he's trippin' off his brother as much as he says he is, but it's his way of gettin' some of your dough. As far as Shante is concerned, my partner, Carlos, is one hundred percent sure that G has her somewhere. G's posse is real tight, so Carlos don't think nobody will slip up and tell where she is. He suggest that we get as much money as we can together, and take it to G. Says he's not the kind of nigga who will turn down no money, and the best we can do is get someone like this fool off your back."

I frowned the whole time Raylo was talking. "At this point, all I care about is Mama. Can somebody just tell me if she's alive? That's all I want to know, and as soon as I know that, we can work out the money thing."

"Prince, I know how you are, but you can't be callin' the shots all the time. Sometimes you gotta play by other people's rules, especially if they're the ones holdin' all the cards. We don't want nothin' to happen to Shante, and since we're workin' with five days, I'd say a li'l cooperation is needed. Now, I got some ideas about gettin' some more money, and I'm willin' to do whatever I gotta do to come up with somethin' on my end. I know you said that you wasn't workin' with what his demands were, but with niggas like G, word is . . . one must do their best to come correct."

"I . . . I can swing about seventy-five . . . maybe a hundred. After that, I'd have to start diggin' deep, sellin' and pawnin' some things to get the rest."

Raylo looked around, making sure that no one was watching us. He took a chunk out of his Big Mac, then wiped his mouth. "I know where I can get the money from, but I may need your help. Can I count on it?"

"I guess it depends on what it is. I'm not gon' rob no banks or nothin' like that, but what you talkin' about?"

"This nigga I know, Ernie Wells, won the lottery. He got 25.5 million and still lives in the same house. He real tight with his money, and from what I know, a lot of it be kept on him and in his house. I'm just sayin' that maybe we can swing by to see what's up. Nobody got to get hurt, and this way you can keep all the money you got, and we can take G the money we get from Ernie. Besides, he won't miss it. With all that jack he's got, a li'l dent in his pockets won't hurt nobody."

I rubbed my hand down my face, really and truly not wanting to go this route again. My entire life had been about robbing, shooting, fighting, and killing. I was tired of that shit, but I knew these cats that had Mama wasn't playing. "Why can't we just take G a hundred grand and see if he'll roll with that? I ain't feelin' that robbery shit, and with that kind of money lying around, you know that brotha got a li'l somethin' for protection. What if we get up in there and get our damn heads blown off? That just seems like a big risk, and when we're so close to havin' all of the money, I don't know if that's a good idea."

"So close? If we go by what you say you got, we still need fifty or seventy-five Gs. Where in the hell dò you think we gon' get it from, the sky? And if you use all of yo' money, then what you gon' do? Close the laundromat and the liquor store? You have to keep up with the rent, don't you? You'll be takin' every dime you got to pay the rent. What you gon' have for yourself? All I'm sayin' is Ernie trusts me. I can get us on the inside, and you can handle it from there. He doesn't know you, and I can say that you're my long-lost son from California."

I still didn't like the plan, but maybe it was my only way. I reached for one of Raylo's fries and put it into my mouth. "Let me sleep on this and get back with you. I just don't know about this, Raylo, I seriously do not know what to do."

"Don't sleep on it for long. Again, time is runnin' out and the next time you go pay that fool G a visit, we go together. He needs to know that you're not in this shit by yourself, and if he thinks about playin' any games, this shit can turn on him in a flash."

I stood up, nodding my head. I told Raylo I would call him early in the morning with my decision.

By the time I got home, I didn't feel like opening up the liquor store, or chilling at the laundromat. I went upstairs, and as I started to knock on Jenay's door to finish what we'd started earlier, I changed my mind about that too. I stuck my key in the door, removed my clothes, and took a long, hot shower. Afterward, I wrapped a towel around my waist and sat on my weight bench. I started to pump iron, growling out loudly each time I strained to raise the heavy bar. I couldn't help but think about what I'd gotten myself into, and about what more was coming my way. Either this thing with Raylo would go smoothly, or there was a possibility that it could all blow up in our faces.

I debated almost all night, doing the math in my head and trying to figure out how much cash I had on hand, and what I could sell to come up with the rest. Truthfully, I had enough, but it would leave me with a couple of thousand that wouldn't go too far after rent was paid on my apartment, the liquor store, and the laundromat. I even thought about selling the laundromat, since it brought in less money than the liquor store. Still, it was money that I needed, so giving up on it didn't make much sense. I wasn't sure what I was going to do, and as it got later, I put on some clothes and sat up on my couch. I rolled a fat-ass joint, sucked in the smoke, and did my best to get high. My whole apartment was infused with the smell of burnt weeds and my eyelids were getting heavy. The heavier they got, my mind started moving in another direction. I closed my eyes, thinking about Poetry standing naked in my apartment earlier today. Daaaaamn, she was sexy, and what in the hell was wrong with me for turning down a chick that fine? She was so sweet in her own little way, and from the first time that I laid eyes on her, I wanted her. Not just sexually, either. I liked that toughness about her and I needed a chick like her who could stand up when something wasn't right. She proved how brave she could be when she confronted fatso that day, she proved how bold she could be when she stepped up and kissed me at Fair St. Louis, and she also proved to me that she was a fighter; that when she wanted something she had no problem going after it. I liked that about her, and even though my life was fucked up right now, maybe she was what I needed.

Then again, maybe it was this fire-ass weed talking for me. I was filling my head with a bunch of nonsense, wasn't I? A woman would run if she knew about what I'd done or what I was capable of doing. There were times that I had no mercy for people who fucked me over, and that included women. Poetry wouldn't dare want to be a part of my life, but she really didn't have to know about all of it, did she?

With that in mind, I reached for my phone and pulled Poetry's number from my pocket. I dialed her number, assuming it was she who answered.

"Poetry," I said.

"Who is this?"

"Prince."

"Who?"

"You heard me. Where you at?"

"At home. Are you coming over?"

"If you still want me to."

"I want you to, only if you didn't make it your business to hook up with Jenay when you got back home. I wouldn't be down with that, and you can forget coming over here if you got your rocks off with her tonight."

I laughed and shook my head. "I didn't go there tonight. When I got back, all I did was shower, lift some weights, and think about you."

She laughed, then went silent. "Bullshit. You wasn't thinking about me. And if you were, swear it. And when you get here I'ma make you pinky swear it, too. You better be telling the truth."

I blushed a little, knowing that she was smiling on the other end. "I was, ma. You know I was. Now, stop talkin' so much and give me your address."

"I will, once you swear it."

"Okay, I swear I didn't go to Jenay's apartment tonight and I've been sitting here thinkin' 'bout you. Now, stop playin' and up the directions."

Poetry gave me her address. I told her I'd be there within the hour.

Deciding to drive my motorcycle that was parked in my landlord's garage, I weaved in and out of traffic down Union Boulevard and on to Page. Poetry's house was to my left. It was an old red brick house that had a big porch. A swing was on the porch and the concrete steps were painted gray. Dressed in my pressed Levi's and a blue tank shirt that hugged my muscles, I removed my helmet and stepped up to the porch. The screen door was hanging off the hinges, so instead of opening it to knock, I rang the tiny doorbell next to the door. Poetry opened the door wearing her faded, torn jeans and a yellow spaghetti-strap top that showed her midriff.

"This is a miracle," she said, blushing. "I can't believe you're here for real. Let me pinch you to make sure it's really you."

I cracked a tiny smile, cocking my head back. "I told you to stop playin', didn't I?"

Poetry squinted, then moved her face close to mine. She lifted my tinted shades and shook her head. "You high as hell, ain't you? Your eyes are red as fire. I should have known that you were on something when you called me."

"Are you goin' to invite me in, or make me stand outside?"

Poetry came outside, closing the door behind her. It was almost eight o'clock, and even though the sun had gone down, it wasn't completely dark yet.

"I would invite you in, but my grandmother just went to sleep. She don't like to be interrupted by people talking, and if we pass by the living room, we'll wake her up. We can stay out here on the porch, but I can go inside to get you something to drink if you want something."

"Nah, I'm good," I said, sitting on the swing. "I guess this way I can keep an eye on my bike, and make sure nobody don't try to steal it."

Poetry looked at my bike, then sat on the swing with me. "That's a really nice bike, but I like your Camaro. What year is it?"

"2010. I bought it brand new, but I didn't feel like drivin' it tonight. My motorcycle is much better, though. And you'll think so too, after I take you for a ride."

Poetry pulled her head back. "You won't be taking me for no ride. I'm scared of those things. They make me nervous."

"I can't believe you're scared of anything, and even if you are, you'll be safe with me. Come on," I said, standing up and putting on my helmet. She hesitated, but agreed to let me take her for a ride.

I helped Poetry straddle my bike, then took my helmet off and put it on her head. "What you gon' use for your big head?" she said, laughing. "Don't you need a helmet too?"

"I do, but I'll be all right. Just hang on tight and don't let go."

I got on my motorcycle, and as soon as I started it up, Poetry grabbed me tight. "Prince, don't be driving all fast and stuff. Go slow, all right?"

"Sure," was all I said. I revved up the engine, doing a U-turn on Page Boulevard, heading west. At first, at the request of Poetry, I went slow. But when her grip loosened up, I started flying down Page. The wind was hitting us with a mild force, and as I weaved in and out of lanes, Poetry squeezed tighter.

"Oh my God," she yelled. "Prince, slow the hell dooooooown!"

I took off, breezing through the green lights that gave me the go ahead, and ignoring Poetry's screams. "Damn it!" she yelled. "Look . . . look at that caaar coming! It's not gon' stooooop!"

I saw the car, but I had the green light, so I kept it moving. Poetry wasn't about to loosen her grip, but she kept pressing her head against my back and screaming. She got so mad at me for going so fast that she bit the shit out of me. That made me go even faster, and as we reached a red light on Skinker, that's when I finally stopped. "I'm getting off of this thing and walking home," she shouted. "You are going too damn fast and I'm not trying to die on this thing with you. This is too much and I'ma bite yo' ass again if you go any faaaaaaster!"

I took off, zooming down the street so fast that if you blinked you missed us. "Prince, this shit ain't funny!" Poetry yelled at the top of her lungs. "I'm going to throw up, and when I do, I'ma do it right on top of your head!"

I still didn't slow down, as going this fast was fun and gave me one hell of a rush. Yeah, it was dangerous, but I liked living on the edge. And whether Poetry was willing to admit it or not, I could tell she was enjoying herself, or, at least, I hoped.

Ready to turn around, I cut over Pennsylvania Avenue and picked up speed. I knew the cops in this area were known for tripping, but I didn't see any so I kept it moving. This time, though, a car that was coming our way cut in front of me. As fast as I was going, I couldn't stop. "Jesus, save me please!" Poetry yelled. "I will never get on this bike with this damn fool again, Lord, and it was so stupid of me tooooooooooooo!"

I quickly swerved in the other lane, causing the motorcycle to lean. And instead of squeezing my waist, Poetry grabbed my dick. She squeezed that motha so tight, it caused my eyes to bug. "Slow this damn thing down," she said, yanking on my package. That shit really did hurt, and the speed of the motorcycle jumped from ninety-five mph to thirty-five mph in an instant. After that, I pulled over, because my dick was hurting.

"That is not how you get me to slow down!" I said, holding myself down below. "I almost flipped this motherfucka over and yo' ass is lucky that I didn't."

She pulled the helmet off her head. Beads of sweat were on her forehead and she wiped them with her hand. "I had to do what was necessary for you to slow this thing down. Have you lost your mind? I thought you were going to go nice and slow with me on the back of here, and who in the hell do you think I am? Some kind of biker bitch or something? This is my first time on one of these things, and I'm about to have a serious heart attack."

"You ain't no fun," I said, taking the helmet from her hand. "I figured you would like the rush and with all of that yellin' and screamin' you was doin', I know that shit felt good."

"If you want me to yell and scream, come up with something better. I know you can, and it shouldn't have nothing to do with this bike."

I smiled from the thoughts of making Poetry yell and scream like I *really* wanted her to. She smiled too, and

I assumed she had read my mind. "Let's go get somethin' to eat," I said. "I'm hungry, what about you?"

"I could eat a li'l something. What you got in mind?"

"You ever eat at the Fried Rice Kitchen in Wellston? They shit be off the chain. Let's stop there."

"I've had them before. I'm down with that, but please do me one favor. I assume you already know what it is, but just in case you don't, please do not go over thirty miles per hour."

"Thirty?" I shouted. "That defeats the purpose of bein' on a motorcycle. I can do forty for you, but no less than that."

She took the helmet from me, putting it back on her head. "I guess I can work with that, but if you go past that, I'm squeezing the Charmin again. Hard."

Poetry hugged my waist again, and as I made my way down Pennsylvania Avenue going slow, she started rubbing my chest. "See what happens when you play by the rules?" she said. Her hands eased up my chest and she rubbed and softly squeezed at my muscles. "You know you hooked up right, Prince. Your skin so soft and you cut in all the right places. Umph, umph, umph," she said and kept on rubbing. When we got to the stoplight to make a right on Dr. Martin Luther King Drive I turned my head to the side.

"You pretty damn hooked up right too," I said. "But if I can recall something that you said awhile back, you said my package wasn't capable of satisfyin' you, didn't you? I hope like hell you don't have to eat your words."

She giggled. "I said that to hurt your feelings, but I wasn't talking about your package right now. I was talking about your chest, so don't be trying to change the subject."

I took off, slowing it down so Poetry would enjoy herself. When we got to the Fried Rice Kitchen, we both went inside to order. Several people stood along the wall, waiting for their orders. I asked Poetry what she wanted, and hated to pull out my stash of money in front of everybody to pay for our food.

"I'll take a half order of shrimp fried rice with gravy and a strawberry Vess soda."

I ordered our food and carefully watched my back as I flipped through the stash in my hand. I paid, then hurried to put the wad back into my pocket. Always being paranoid about my surroundings, I waited for our food outside with Poetry. We stood by my bike talking while our food got ready.

"You know you never told me how old you are," I said. "Where do you work, and do you have any kids?"

"I never told you because every time I get close to you, you ran away. I'm twenty-one, don't have no kids, and if I had a job do you think I'd be begging you for one? I've been trying to find one, though, but it's been kind of rough for me because I dropped out of school and never got my GED. That's one of the real reasons I've been bugging you at the laundromat and I need some money. Besides, you need somebody to handle your business for you, 'cause you so unfriendly that you're going to drive people away."

"I take it you're being funny, but why you drop out of school? I did too, but I was still able to do some things to put me on the right track. I dropped out because I couldn't get along with my coach and school didn't challenge me no more."

"I dropped out because I was having some family problems. My mother is . . . was a crackhead and she made my life so damn miserable. I wound up moving in with my grandmother and she's been taking care of me for years. Then I had a situation where my uncle kept trying to hit on me, and when I ran away, I met this dude named Anthony who I thought really cared for me. I caught him cheating on me, then he went off to the army and married somebody else. My whole world was turned upside down and school was the last place I wanted to be. I regret not going back, but I am going to someday get my GED."

It seemed like Poetry had been through some shit too, and I was sure there was nothing worse than having a crackhead for a parent. "Where your father at? And maybe we can work somethin' out about you workin' for me."

Poetry smiled, then rolled her eyes. "I hope we can work something out, but as for my father, I have no idea who he is. My mother was all over the place and ain't no telling what man out here laid a seed in her to have me. All I know is I was born in Alabama, and I guess he still lives there. He probably don't know nothing about me, but even if he did, I'm not sure if it really matters. For years, it's just been me and my grandmother. She's the only mother I know and will forever know."

Her situation reminded me too much of Romeo's, except his mother was in jail. His grandmother died a few months before he was sentenced, but he counted on her, just like Poetry seemed to count on her grandmother. My mind had eased a bit from all that was going on with me, but as Poetry and I talked about family, I couldn't help but think about Mama. Damn, what was I going to do? I had put the only way out of this with Raylo behind me for now, but there it was staring me right in the face. Thank God for Poetry helping me to clear my mind tonight as I tried to focus on her alone.

We got our food that was put into a brown paper bag. I slowly drove back to Poetry's house, and as we rode, she laid her head against my back. Her hands continued to stroke my chest, and I'd be lying if I said her touch didn't feel good. When I pulled in front of her house, she got off my bike and removed the helmet. She reached for her box of rice and told me she would be right back. I waited for her to return, and since I was hot, I pulled my shirt over my head and tucked part of it into my back pocket. I removed my box of rice from the bag, assuming that Poetry had gone inside to get us some forks, even though plastic ones were in the bag. When she came back outside, she was empty-handed. She straddled my bike again, and I turned around to face her.

"Where your food at?" I asked.

"I gave it to my grandmother."

"Why you didn't ask me to buy her somethin'? Now, what you gon' eat?"

"I'ma eat some of yours," she said, watching me open my box. Steam from the gravy ran across our noses, smelling damn good.

"Unfortunately, ma, you ain't got nothin' comin'. All of this rice here is goin' in my stomach and my stomach only."

I started to eat my rice, teasing Poetry as if it was so good. It really was, so I didn't have to pretend. "Mmmm," I said with each bite. "Delicious."

Poetry playfully pushed my shoulder. "Oooo, you are so wrong, Prince. Give me some. Just a little."

I kept teasing Poetry, then reached out to give her some of my rice. When she opened her mouth, I snatched the fork away and put it into my mouth. We both laughed, and to be honest, I couldn't remember the last time I laughed so hard about anything. Poetry pouted and folded her arms. She looked so cute that I couldn't resist sharing my rice.

"I meant to ask you," she said after she swallowed the rice. "I know your real name ain't Prince, is it?"

"Yes. It's Jamal Prince Perkins, but don't you ever call me Jamal. I prefer Prince. Now, what about you? I'm sittin' here sharin' my rice with you and don't remember your last name. I remember seein' it on your driver's license, but what is it?"

"I'm not going to tell you because all you're going to do is laugh."

"Why would I laugh? I don't recall it being that funny."

"My last name is Wright. Poetry Wright, get it?"

I shrugged, but smiled as it came back to me. "Do you *write*, Poetry?"

"See, I knew you'd make fun of my name. I don't write poetry, but I do love to write."

"I do too. But I haven't done so in a while."

Poetry reached out to touch my chest. She scrolled her fingers along my Street Soldier tattoo and looked at my mother's name. "Girlfriend?" she asked.

"Nope. Mama."

"What about Street Solider? What does that mean?"

"It means that I'm a soldier on the streets, particularly in my hood. I see the streets as bein' a warzone and me being a soldier who's learnin' how to survive."

"Then I guess I'm a Street Soldier too. It ain't been no picnic for me, but at least I'm still alive. I guess I can't complain."

"Me either," I said, changing my thoughts to what was really going on with me.

I lost my appetite, and gave Poetry the rest of my rice. She held the box in her hand and started to finish it off. I wrapped my arms around her waist and looked at her still straddled on my bike. "Ay, I apologize for givin' you such a hard time about us hookin' up. Again, I was diggin' you since the first time I saw you, but wasn't sure about how to approach you. You forgive me?"

"Uh huh," she said, looking into the rice box and scrapping the sides with the fork. She put the last of it in her mouth, then closed the box. "Let's go on the porch. I would invite you inside, but truth is, my grandmother be trippin' about people she don't know being in her house."

"I'm good," I said, helping Poetry off my bike. I followed her on the porch and we sat next to each other on the swing.

"So, you gon' give me a job or what?" she asked.

"You are dead serious about finding a job, aren't you?"

"Hell, yeah, I'm serious. Having no money ain't fun, but I guess it depends on how much you paying."

"My pay is always good. Spectacular, some may say, but you can be sure that you'll be well taken care of."

Poetry pursed her lips. "You talking about sex, and I'm talking about money. And you may as well get your mind out of the gutter, because you ain't getting none of this booty no time soon."

"For real?" I said with a shocked look on my face. "You seriously ain't gon' give me none? You were so willin' to earlier, and now you done already changed your mind?"

"I wasn't going to give you none earlier. I was just messing with you. Wanted you to see what you were missing out on, and I guess it worked. If you had opted to do it, I would have changed my mind and left."

"See, you be playin' too much. How you gon' get naked in front of me, then not be willin' to up the goods? You know I want some of that pretty pussy and that shit did look good."

Poetry blushed, then pushed me back as I tried to move closer to her. I grabbed her waist and pulled her close to me. "Let's go back to my apartment so I can hit that," I said. "You know you want to feel me, don't you?"

Poetry pulled away from me and shook her head. "Uh, no. I told you you weren't getting none, especially how you played me. It's going to be a loooong time before we get down like that. I hope you're willing to wait."

"Wait for what? I'm horny as hell right now!" I grabbed my crotch. "You would be so wrong for makin' me wait."

Poetry shrugged. "Sorry. But you played yourself today. And if you want to go back to your place and get served by that stripper-looking chick, go right ahead."

After Poetry turning me down, it wasn't like the thought of being with Jenay hadn't crossed my mind. But I was enjoying my time with Poetry, and when she laid her head across my lap, I really felt comfortable.

"Don't you go to sleep," I said. "I know I'm not that borin', am I?"

"Not at all. I had fun today, even though you damn near killed us on your bike."

"You were in good hands. I wasn't goin' to let anything happen to you."

As those words left my mouth, I became quiet. I hoped that if our connection turned into something, I could always protect her from harm. I hadn't done a good job of protecting the ones I cared about, and if this ever became a difficult task for me, I knew I had to let go. We continued our conversation on the porch until almost two in the morning. I kept yawning, and when Poetry walked with me to my bike, I held her hand.

"I'll call you soon," I said.

"You'd better. Get some rest, and thanks for the good time."

We both leaned in at the same time, tearing up each other's lips. My hands roamed and so did hers. Holding her ass in my hands felt good, and as my dick started to rise, I hated to go there with her again, but couldn't help it. "Come on and go back to my apartment with me. I'll make it so worth it."

"I'm sure you will, but I want to wait. I hope you don't mind. You kind of wishy-washy, Prince, and I don't want to be that chick who you just run to to get a nut. I'm looking for something more than that."

I nodded, but wasn't sure if I was ready to give Poetry the kind of relationship she wanted. And instead of begging for it, I took off on my bike, rushing home to take a cold shower.

I lay naked in bed, thinking about her and about the decision I had finally made about setting up Raylo's friend. It had to be done, and as far as I could see it, there really was no other way.

# Chapter Nine

### Friends . . .
### How Many of Us Really Have Them?

Yesterday I spoke to Raylo, telling him I was down with his plan. He wanted me to meet him at Mama's house around seven tonight so we could go to Ernie's house together. I didn't have a good feeling about this, but the way Raylo said we could get away with it sounded doable. I checked on Nate at the liquor store, made sure everything was calm at the laundromat, then drove to Mama's house to meet Raylo.

As soon as I got there, my cell phone rang. I looked at it only to see Poetry's number. Since the other night, she'd called me two of three times, but I had been very busy with trying to take care of this thing with Mama. I told her that once I was finished handling some business today, I would stop by to see her. According to her, her grandmother had left for Mississippi to visit some relatives and would be gone for a couple of days. I was anxious to see her, too, but this definitely came first. I let her call go to voice mail, then went inside to meet Raylo. The door was already open. He stood in the living room, guzzling down a frothy bottle of beer. He pulled the bottle away from his lips, then held it out to me.

"You want one?" he asked. "There's plenty in the fridge."

"Nah, I'm good. Ready to get this show on the road, I think."

Raylo cocked his head back. "You think?"

For whatever reason, what I had done to Monroe was on my mind. I hadn't mentioned any of it to Raylo, and before we went to his partner's house, I decided to bring up the subject of Monroe, just to see Raylo's reaction.

"I mean, I just got a funny feeling inside about some things. Do you happen to know a man by the name of Monroe who Mama dated?"

"Monroe?" he asked, putting the beer bottle up to his lips again. He swallowed, then shook his head. "Hell nah, I don't know no nigga named Monroe. And when was she supposed to be seeing him when she's been with me for years?"

Raylo looked offended by the mention of Monroe's name. I didn't notice anything out of the ordinary, but I pushed. "I heard her mention him before and I figured she may be somewhere with him. Especially if she's upset with you, it only makes sense for her to run to her other man."

"There better not had been another man," he said, raising his voice. "Do you know where this nigga live? 'Cause we can stop by his house right now to see what's up!"

"Nah, I only know where he lives. I know where he used to live, but I've already been there. Jus' . . . just thought you may know him or somethin'. No big deal."

"It may not be a big deal to you, but I know damn well Shante better not be shacked up with another motherfucker somewhere. After putting me through all of this bullshit, worryin' about her ass, I will hurt her if she's been with another man all along. That's on a for real tip right there."

I said nothing else, and watched as Raylo finished off his beer. I guess I believed him, for now, and whether I liked it or not, it was time to take care of business. Dressed in jeans, a plaid-like button-down shirt, and dress shoes, Raylo started toward Mama's bedroom. "I'll be right back," he said. "Do you got that handy?"

I knew he was referring to my Glock .23, so I raised my T-shirt so he could see it stuffed inside of my black Levis. A cap was on my head, as I tried to hide as much of myself as I could. Raylo rubbed his hands together, then left the room. He came back with his piece, tucking it behind him and ready to go. I followed him outside, and after he locked the door we made our way to his car.

"What in the fuck is that smell?" I said, wondering if it was his cologne.

"I don't smell nothin'."

"Whatever it is, it's strong as hell. Make me want to throw the hell up."

Raylo sniffed the air, then looked over at the neighbors. We saw smoke coming from behind some trees. "They over there barbecuin'. Smells pretty damn good to me."

"Not to me. They should be shot for cookin' meat that smells that bad."

Raylo laughed and we got in his Cadillac and left. The ride to his so-called friend's house was quiet, but I sparked up a conversation to get as much information as I could out of Raylo.

"Tell me somethin', Raylo. Why were you and your friend followin' me that day I was at the gas station? I know you saw me coming after y'all, but what was up with that?"

Raylo hesitated to answer, then he came clean. "Believe it or not, young blood, I'm uneasy right now. This thing

with yo' Mama got me on edge and I've been watchin' my
back and everybody else's. While you think I may have
been involved in her disappearance, at the time I wasn't
so sure about you. I had to keep my ears and eyes open, if
you know what I mean."

I pointed to my chest. "So, in other words, you're sayin' that you thought I had somethin' to do with Mama
disappearin'."

"What I'm sayin' is I trust no one. You be doin' some
fucked-up shit, Prince, and I don't know if you comin'
or goin' sometimes. Like I said, and no offense, but I
must pay attention to my surroundings."

"I get all of that, but why in the hell would I do somethin' to my own mama? I ain't never had no beef with
her about nothin' that severe where I would want to
make her disappear. It's fucked up that you thinkin'
like that and you're damn right I'm offended."

Raylo stopped at the red light, then reached over to
touch my heaving chest. I was very upset . . . about to
renege on what we was about to do, because I wasn't
feeling what he was saying to me. "Calm down, all
right? Truth is, I miss yo' mama, Prince. It's drivin' me
crazy because I can't find her. I try not to let what I'm
goin' through show, but this shit is eatin' me up. The
way she left out . . . upset with me and arguin' and shit,
don't make me feel good. I don't know where she could
be right now and all I'm thinkin' about is our last conversation. It wasn't good. And whether you believe me
or not, I'm a nigga with a heart too. I cared deeply for
yo' mama and it would crush me if somethin' has happened to her and we went out the way we did."

I started thinking about me and Mama's last conversation too. It was cool, but she did ask me to bring
her some things and I refused to do it. Of course, now I
was regretting it. Maybe not as much as Raylo was and

I was so sure that argument they had was pretty darn heated. "I guess I get what you're saying, man, but the last thing I would do is hurt my mama. She's pissed me the fuck off, plenty of times, but you were barkin' up the wrong tree with me."

"And just to let you know . . . you're barkin' up the wrong tree with me. I'm with you on this. She pissed me the fuck off a lot too, but I ain't never loved a woman as much as I love Shante. We like this," he said, crossing his fingers tightly. "And ain't nothin' gon' change that."

I nodded and kept looking straight ahead. I wasn't sure who or what to believe right now, but G had to get his money and then maybe that would shed some light on this fucked-up situation that was starting to drive me nuts.

Ernie lived in North County in a subdivision known as Hathaway Manor. With me being born and raised in North City, I rarely made my way to the county unless I had gone to one of the football games back in the day. It wasn't as if the area was upscale or anything like that, and most of the county was now populated with blacks. Many of those who lived in the city made their way to North County, only because the houses were much bigger and retail business was booming. Years ago, Mama had talked about making a move to North County, but as I saw many just like me lurking around, I was glad she hadn't.

Raylo pulled in front of a long, ranch-style house that looked to be well kept. We had already discussed how things would go down, so we both got out of the car, prepared to take care of business. After Raylo rang the doorbell, Ernie opened it with a smile, appearing to be glad to see his so-called friend.

"Why yo' ass been hidin' out?" Ernie asked Raylo and invited us in. "I haven't seen you in like six months, nigga. I thought you had moved."

"Nah," Raylo said. "Just been keepin' things on the low-low. I stopped all that sellin' shit and decided to chill." Raylo looked at me, and tapped my chest. "This here my li'l nigga from California. You remember Justine, don't you?"

Ernie looked as if he was in thought and slowly shook his head. "Yeah, I remember Justine. Is this what came of that?"

"No doubt," Raylo said. "This is my son, Clay. He hangin' out with me today and I wanted to show him that all of my partners ain't losers." They both laughed and Ernie reached out to shake my hand. He had a tight-ass grip, and was a pretty big dude, too. Looked like a linebacker, and I wasn't sure if I would be able to take him down.

"Nice to meet you," I said, looking around at the okay house that had old-time furniture. For someone who had won the lottery, I sure as hell couldn't tell. Raylo said he was cheap, but damn. "You got a nice place," I lied. "Real nice."

Ernie seemed proud, and started to show me and Raylo around. Raylo had been to his house before, so he told me to pay attention to certain things during our tour. He knew Ernie was going to showcase some shit and that he did. The liveliness of the house didn't happen until we reached the finished basement. That's where the money was spent. He had wide-screen TVs on the wall, leather chairs and a sofa, a glass bar with every kind of liquor you could think of behind it, and a walk-out sliding door that led to an Olympic-sized swimming pool in the backyard. Waterfall-rock landscaping was on each side and the shit was hooked up real nice. Another thing that his money had been spent on was his cars. The four-car garage that we walked to housed a Bentley, Cadillac, a '65 Lincoln Continental, and a Lamborghini. The garage that was attached to his house had a motorcycle inside and a Lexus SUV that he drove every day.

Ernie went on and on about his good fortune, not having no idea as to what was about to happen. We went back inside, sitting in the leather chairs in the basement.

"Can I get y'all anything to drink?" he asked me and Raylo.

"Clay ain't drinkin' nothin', but you can get me a shot of rum and Coke."

Ernie went to the bar, making him and Raylo some drinks. When he came over to us, he handed Raylo his drink, then gave me a cooler. "To hell with what yo' daddy says, I think you may want a li'l somethin'-somethin' too."

I smiled and thanked him for being kind. As he and Raylo started to talk, I watched a movie that was playing on the TV. I pretended to be all into it, but my mind was focused on making my next move. Nearly fifteen minutes had elapsed before I stood up and yawned.

"Ernie, do you have a bathroom down here?" I asked.

"Yeah, it's over there in that corner." He pointed to it. "If there ain't no soap on the sink to wash yo' hands, look in one of those closets and you should be able to find some."

"Thanks," I said, making my way to the bathroom. This was how Raylo and I had planned it. As soon as I returned, I was supposed to make my move. A huge part of me was nervous, though. I hadn't done no shit like this in months and Ernie was someone I never had no beef with. He seemed like a really nice man who didn't deserve what was about to happen to him. Still, I realized that I needed to hurry up and get this the fuck over with so Mama could get back and this mess could be behind us.

I flushed the toilet, then washed my hands and dried them with a towel. Right then, my cell phone vibrated and it was Poetry calling me again. I sighed and quickly answered.

"Yeah," I said, irritated by her numerous calls.

"Are you still coming over tonight?"

"I said I was, didn't I?"

"Yes, but what time, Prince? It's already seven-thirty. I thought you'd be here by now."

"It'll probably be much later, but I'll get there when I can. Now, I gotta go. In a minute."

I hung up and made my way back to the sitting area where Raylo and Ernie were. Ernie's back was to me, and Raylo could see me coming their way. I pulled my Glock from my pants and carefully placed it on the back of Ernie's head.

"Don't move," I said. "If you do, I'ma have to blow a hole in your brain."

Ernie looked frozen and didn't even look as if he was breathing.

Raylo started to take part in the act and jumped up from his seat. "Nigga, what you doin'?" he yelled at me. "Put that damn gun down before somebody get hurt!"

"Sit the fuck down or else I'll shoot yo' ass too! I need some motherfuckin' money, and either you or him gon' give it to me!"

"You . . . you can have whatever you want," Ernie said, shaking with his hands up. "Just don't kill me."

I pushed the gun upside his head while holding tight on to the back of his shirt. Raylo kept with his bullshit that was coming off too damn fake for me. "Clay, don't do this man. Let that man go and let's get the fuck out of here. You don't have to do this, and why in the fuck would you come to my partner's house and pull some shit like this!"

I ignored Raylo, and asked Ernie where his money was. He was sweating bullets and did his best to remain calm.

"Be . . . behind the bar. Open the bottom cabinet, and inside of there is a safe. The combination is 36-25-14-90. You can take whatever is inside."

Right now was when I was supposed to shoot Ernie in the head, but I told Raylo I was against it. He side-eyed me and took a deep breath. I kept with my own plan, and instead, I lifted the gun and cracked Ernie hard against the back of his head. He touched his head and blood was on his fingers. "Please," he begged as I hit him again, this time staggering him to the floor. The last blow knocked him out cold. He fell flat on the floor and didn't move. The open gash on the back of his head was gushing with blood, but I still didn't believe he was dead. Raylo and I rushed over to the bar. We opened the cabinet and saw the safe that Ernie had mentioned.

"Hurry up and open it," Raylo said.

I remembered the combination, but after trying it three times, the damn thing wouldn't open.

"Take your time," Raylo said, breathing heavy. "36, 25, 14, then 90."

I tried again, no luck. Raylo pushed me aside, then tried himself. He didn't have any luck either.

"Damn it," he shouted. "I know that motherfucka didn't lie, did he?"

Raylo started to panic and so did I. "You was supposed to shoot to kill that nigga!" he shouted. "Now we gotta go search for some shit and I don't want to leave this fool lyin' here with breath still in him. Go take that fool out so we can go find what we came here for."

Just then, my phone rang. I knew it was Poetry by the sound of the ringtone. I wanted to curse her ass out for constantly calling me, and as nervous as I was right now, I could have hurt somebody. Thing was, I didn't want it to be Ernie. "Fuck it," I said to Raylo. "I don't want to be runnin' around here ransackin' this nigga's crib all night. We were supposed to be in and out of here and that shit wasn't in the plans."

"Neither was knockin' him upside his fuckin' head. Now, go do like I told you to. I'ma go upstairs to see what I can find."

I wasn't one to take orders, and Raylo knew it. My face twisted as I stood mean mugging his ass. "I'm not killin' no damn body. I said it's time to switch to plan B, so let's go!"

Ernie squirmed around on the floor, then turned over to lie on his back. He was out of it, but was definitely alive. Raylo snatched my gun from on top of the safe, then went over to Ernie. He stood over him, and without hesitation, pumped two right into his head. Ernie's body wiggled, then his breathing stopped. Some of his blood splattered on Raylo, and with each shot, my whole body jumped.

"Help me get the goddamn safe and let's carry it out of here," he said. "That's the least you can do. I hope you ain't too chicken to help me carry the damn thing."

None of this was sitting right with me, but I went ahead and helped Raylo carry the heavy safe to the car. I waited outside while he went back in, wiping down a few things and bringing his drinking glass with him. He tossed my gun into my lap and slammed the car door.

"This is why I don't fuck with scary-ass niggas like you," he said, backing up and speeding out of Ernie's driveway.

I didn't even respond. We drove back to Mama's house in silence, and when we got there, we both carried the safe inside. Raylo put it on the coffee table and sat on the couch. I stood next to it, watching as he took several deep breaths before attempting to open the safe again. Still no luck.

"I can't believe this shit!" he said. "Damn!"

"I'm sure we can get somebody to open it, so what's the big deal?"

Raylo cocked his head back and looked at me as if I called him out of his name. "If I have to take this safe to somebody, then they'll want a piece of what's inside. Not only that, they'll question me about how I got it. I don't know about you, but I don't tell niggas out here everything I do. Now, we need to figure out how to get this damn thing open, as I'm sure everything we need to get your mama back, and then some, is inside."

I let out a deep sigh, then sat next to Raylo on the couch. I kept trying and trying to open the safe, and when I heard it click, we eyeballed each other. Nervous, I slowly pulled on the heavy door and looked inside. That's when I got the shock of my life, as the damn thing was empty. Raylo stuck his hand inside, then slammed his fist on top of it.

"Ain't this about a bitch! I told you we should've searched his house, didn't I!"

I was speechless, as our plan had failed—big time.

"We need to go back over there and see what else we can get!" Raylo suggested. "I'm not goin' out like this, and Shante will die if we don't come up with G's money! Are you with me in this or not?"

I wiped my eyes and squeezed my forehead. My head was banging and this was too damn much for me to deal with right now. "I'm not goin' back to that man's house. I'm sure that somebody heard those shots and the police may already be there. You can go back, but I already know what I gotta do. I'm goin' to go see G in the mornin'. I'll pay him what I got and we can go from there."

I got up and walked out. Raylo continued to talk shit, but I tuned him out.

"You ol' scary-ass nigga," he yelled. "Prince, you ain't shit! I thought yo' ass was about somethin'! Let's go back over there and get what we can. Come on!"

I kept on moving. If Raylo decided to go with me tomorrow, cool. If not, so be it.

All I really wanted to do was go home and lay back until tomorrow. But since I didn't want to upset Poetry, I was on my way to her house. Either way, it was time for G to tell me what was up with Mama, and, hopefully, the money that I'd give him would be enough. After all was said and done, I had $90,000 that I could give him and still keep some for myself. I hoped like hell it would be enough, and if not, I just had to chalk it all up and be completely broke.

I parked my car in front of Poetry's house, slowly making my way to the door with my head hanging low. Ernie's dead body kept flashing before me, and so were my thoughts of Mama. Raylo had sent me a text, telling me not to make a move to G's place without him. Said he'd be at my place by nine in the morning, and since it was almost eleven at night, I wasn't sure when I'd be able to get some rest.

Poetry opened the door wearing a baby doll satin white bustier corset with matching G-string panties. A garter held up her white stockings and when she turned around, all ass was in my view. Her tiny breasts barely filled the top of the corset, but she looked sexy as hell. I walked in, closing the door behind me, almost in shock. A staircase was right there, leading to the upper level. But Poetry had made her way to the left, which was the living room. Several scented candles were lit throughout, the couch was pulled out into a neatly made bed, chilled wine in a bucket was on the table, and the melodies of Trey Songz were kicking it up in the background. Poetry kneeled on the floor next to the table and started to pour a glass of wine. "It's about time," she said, holding the flute glass out to me. "Come in and have a seat. Don't be scared. I promise I won't bite."

As gorgeous as she looked, and after all of her efforts, I was not with this tonight. I didn't know whether to tell her now or tell her later. I walked sluggishly into the room, keeping my hands in my pockets. I stood next to her, and as she looked up at me with those pretty hazel-green eyes, I touched the side of her face. She was so damn pretty, and in no way did I deserve to have a chick like her in my life. I knew it, but didn't know how to say it. Instead, I leaned down, planting a soft kiss on her lips. The taste was so sweet, and as our tongues intertwined she rose to her feet. I eased my arms around her waist and my hands lowered to squeeze her bare ass. It was damn sure meaty and I had a handful.

"Take your clothes off," she whispered. "Or, do you want me to do it?"

After touching and kissing her, I was so sure my mind would clear. But the more I tried, I started feeling as if I was having an anxiety attack, thinking about what had just happened and Mama. I backed away from Poetry, and rubbed my face hard with my hands.

"I'm sorry, ma, but I . . . I have got to get out of here." I turned to walk away.

Poetry reached out for my arm, grabbing it. "What's up with you, Prince?" Frustration as well as confusion was all over her face. Her brows arched inward and her eyes watered. "I can't believe you're getting ready to walk out of here without giving me an explanation as to why."

I pulled my arm away from her grip, wanting so badly to tell her what was going on, but couldn't. "I just need to go," I said. "Don't take it personal."

I walked to the door and Poetry followed me outside. She was mad as hell, and quite frankly, I couldn't blame her. "Why, Prince?" she yelled as I got in my car. She held the door so I wouldn't close it. I avoided her by looking straight ahead. "What the fuck is wrong with you? I go through all of this, just for you, and this is how you play me! You need to tell me what the fuck is up, or don't worry about calling me again!"

Several horns blew, and some fools were yelling out the window at Poetry. "Goddamn!" one brotha shouted and whistled.

Another actually stopped his car, "Daaaaamn, sexy, you need a ride?"

Poetry rolled her eyes, telling him, "No, thank you."

He slowly drove away, but she couldn't get another word out because niggas kept driving by, hollering out at her. "How much?" one man stopped to say.

I had had enough and that's when I turned to her. "Would you go inside before I have to get out of my car and hurt somebody? I can't tell you what's goin' on right now, but I will do so soon. I thank you for goin' all out like this tonight, but I need to go."

Poetry stood for a moment, staring at me. All she did was shake her head, then ran off to go inside. I watched as she closed the door, then turned off the porch light. I felt bad for what I had done, and the whole damn day had been fucked up. Hopefully, after tomorrow, I'd be able to piece my life back together and stop it from spiraling out of control.

# Chapter Ten

## The Girl Is Mine,
## Even Though I Don't Want Her To Be . . .

Raylo and I sat face-to-face with G in his living room. He had just counted the money, and along with Raylo's $5,000, we had presented him with $95,000 for the safe return of Mama.

"What say you?" Raylo said to G as he sat in silence. "It's all we could come up with and I'ma need you to make a move and tell us where Shante is."

G yawned, then sat back on the couch. "I don't know why you and soldier boy believe y'all can come over here and tell me what to do, when you don't have the money that I asked for, nor do you have the prize in your possession. The money you niggas brought me is chump change, and I need a few minutes to see if I can work with this."

"You can, and you will," Raylo charged. "Now, if I have to make arrangements to pay the rest to you later, I will. But you need to know that it ain't easy comin' up with the kind of money you asked for. We gave you all that we had and it's gon' have to be enough!"

"Slow yo' roll, Ray. I'll decide if it'll be enough, and if I decide to make arrangements with you about gettin' the rest of it later, yo' ass betta pay up. If you don't, I got a whole lot of niggas out there antsy about puttin' you and your Street Soldier to rest. Now, sit for a minute. I'll be right back."

G got up and went into the other room. Raylo turned to me, suggesting that I remain calm and let him do the talking. He could see my leg shaking and he knew that I wanted to get up, blow G's brains out, and call it a day. I was sure Mama would understand, as all of this back and forth bullshit was working my nerves.

Ten minutes later, G came back into the living room with his cell phone pressed against his ear. "Tell that bitch to calm down," he said. "I'm gettin' sick of hearin' her mouth."

"Is that my mama?" I asked, sitting up from my slumped position on the couch. "Let me holla at her, all right?"

G ignored me and kept on talking. Minutes later, he laid the phone down and looked at Raylo. "For now, we got a deal. But every month, until I'm paid up, I need you to bring me a li'l somethin'. The longer you take, the longer this problem lingers on. Once I get all of my money, everybody will be happy, nobody has to know about the dead millionaire in Hathaway Manor, nor about my brother who was slaughtered in a bathroom. We can call it a good day." He swiped his hands together. "And go live happily ever after."

"That's all fine and dandy, but we need to hear from Shante," Raylo said. "Ain't no way in hell I'm leavin' you with all this money, and we don't know where she's at."

G slid the phone across the table to Raylo. "She's where she's been all along," he said. "At home. Call her."

Raylo dialed Mama's phone and put the phone on speakerphone so I could hear. A man answered and Raylo asked who he was. "Don't worry about it," he said. "Here, bitch, say somethin'."

"Hello," Mama said. "I'm fine, but please come get—"

"There you have it," the man said and hung up.

Raylo looked at me, but something didn't seem right to me. I guess it didn't seem right to Raylo either, as he dialed the number again. G snatched the phone from his hand. "We're done doin' business," he said. "Don't forget about the rest of my money, and do me a favor: try to enjoy your day. After all, Mama's home."

I got up from my seat, still feeling fucked up inside. All of my money was on the table and would soon be in his hands. Raylo and I moved quickly to his car, running almost every stoplight that we could to get to Mama's house. When we got there, the front door was wide open. I rushed in, yelling for Mama.

"Mama," I yelled, making my way back to her room, since there was no sign of her in the living room or kitchen. I got no answer, and when I opened the door to her bedroom, it looked the same as it was before. My stomach dropped, and as I checked my room, the bathroom, and the basement, she wasn't there. I wondered where Raylo was. When I went into the kitchen, that's when I saw him sitting calmly in the kitchen chair with a voice recorder in his hand. He hit the play button, and that's when we heard Mama's voice say what we'd heard earlier and what I'd heard a while back. We'd been set the fuck up! Raylo stood, throwing the recorder into the wall and breaking it. I was so mad that I punched my fist into the wall, causing a gaping hole.

"Where in the fuck is she?" I yelled. A slow tear rolled down my face and I started to lose it. "Damn, Mama, where are you!" I dropped to my knees and my emotions ran over. Raylo stood next to me, gripping my shoulder and squeezing it.

"Hang in there," he said. "Don't go out like this, man, we'll find her."

I wiped the tears and snot from my nose. My body was shaking and I couldn't control myself. "When?" I asked. "When we gon' find her? She probably dead, man. All because of me . . . I know she's dead."

"No, she ain't," Raylo said, still trying to console me. "Let's put our heads together and figure out what we need to do. We ain't goin' out like this and these niggas gonna pay for playin' games with us. First, we need to go back to G's and get our money. I know he ain't gon' let us back in, but he gotta come out some time. And when he does, we need to be prepared to catch his ass and blow some shit up. I'm tired of playin' games, and if somebody has hurt my Shante, those fools gon' pay."

"I'm tired, too. Sick and tired of all of this!" I stood and wiped the tears from my face.

"I know you've been through a lot, Prince. And what I want you to do is go back home and chill. I'ma make some phone calls and hook up with some of my partners. I'll tell them what happened and we gon' case the area where G lives. As soon as I get him, I'll call you so you can come and deal with him personally. This may take some time, as I'm sure him and his goons are expectin' us to run over there right now and deal with them. We gotta be smart, though. Catch 'em unexpectedly. I don't know how Shante is ever goin' to make her way back to us, but we gotta deal with them right now. So sit tight. Don't make no moves unless you consult me first."

I was out of ideas and felt drained. And whatever Raylo came up with, I was down with it. For now, though, I left to go lay my head down for a while as it was hurting so badly.

When I got back to my apartment, my eyes were red and puffy. I pushed the button on the elevator, and as I waited for it to open, I saw Francine hugged up with another one of her sugar daddies. She never did bring me that lasagna, and I guessed since I wasn't down with sucking her pussy, she decided to cut me off. That was fine by me, and as soon as the elevator opened, I got on and headed upstairs. I opened my door, fell back on the couch, and turned again to the man above who really didn't seem to give a damn about me. Why I continued to go there . . . I didn't know.

The constant ringing of my cell phone awakened me. When I looked at it, the time showed 3:15 A.M., and the call was from Raylo. I hurried to answer in a groggy tone. "What's up?"

"Them niggas gone, Prince. We had been watchin' G's place all night until I decided to bombard a woman who lived there and followed her inside. We had to be careful because of the cameras, but when we got to G's door, and kicked it down, the whole damn place was empty. I'm sure they knew we were comin' back and decided to get the hell out of dodge before we did. If he still in the Lou, he will be found. Don't worry, and I promise you we will find that nigga before he gets too far away with our money."

I sat up straight, rubbing my eyes. "What about Mama? Anything on her?"

Raylo was silent for a while, then he spoke up. "One of Shante's nightgowns was found in G's loft. It had bloodstains all over it, and was the same one she wore the night she left. I don't know . . ." He paused.

"All right," I said, wanting to hear no more. "Appreciate the call."

I hung up and dropped my head. I rubbed my hair, trying to squeeze it. All kinds of pain ran through me, and even though Mama's and my relationship hadn't been the best over the years, there was no doubt that I loved her. I would never forgive myself for bringing hurt to her like this, and it was time for me to face the fact that she might not be coming home. I leaned back on the couch, holding my chest and releasing more emotions.


Three weeks had gone by, and Mama or no Mama, the sun was still shining. My life, however, was like living in hell. I couldn't understand my purpose for living and I hated life more than ever. Nate was doing his best to cheer me up, not knowing anything about all that had happened. I kept everything on the hush-hush, because if there ever came a time when I had to make a move and settle things my own way, I didn't want anything to trace back to me. Nate kept pressing me about what was going on with me, but my only explanation was money. It was, indeed, tight, but I was doing whatever to make more of it. That included me asking Poetry to take over for me at the laundromat three days a week. I had overexerted myself, and with so much on my mind, my attitude wasn't that great. I had been going off on my customers, losing business by the day. I figured Poetry could do a much better job than me, and she seemed to get along better with the women who came in to wash.

As for the liquor store, Nate was still handling things well. I didn't want to make any changes with that, because it was the bulk of where my money came from. Freeing up my days at the laundromat gave me time to do my own investigation behind the setup. I'd gone to G's loft myself and, sure enough, he was gone. I asked questions to several people hanging around, but no one knew nothing. I went to some of the local hangouts, trying to see if I saw him anywhere, but had no luck. I wasn't going to give up until I knew what had happened to Mama.

Raylo seemed to stay at it on his end too. He stayed in touch about who he talked to and what kind of leads he had. Nothing checked out as of yet, but one day, soon, either he was going to get a breakthrough or I was.

Nate tossed me a soda before I locked the door to head back over to the laundromat. I had been thinking about downsizing and moving the laundromat to a smaller place. I was on my way to go see the other building, but planned to stop by to tell Poetry I was leaving. She was still upset with me about playing her that night, but when I offered her a job, she jumped on it. I only paid her $200 a week, but that was good enough for her. Nate stopped me on my way out the door.

"If you want me to go check out the building with you I can. I can shut it down here for an hour or so, just to give you my thoughts on if you should change locations," Nate said.

I needed every dime I could get, so closing the store didn't make sense to me. "Nah, I'm good. If I think it may be a good move, I'll let you see it before I sign any papers. I'll check back later."

Nate got back to my customers and I left. As I walked across the street, I saw Poetry standing outside with a dude wearing army gear. Black boots were on his feet and a cap was lowered on his bald head. He was leaned against a blue Saturn. I remembered her mentioning her ex-boyfriend, Anthony, who had dissed her and married someone else. I wondered if it was him. Poetry was all smiles as she looked at him, and whatever he was saying to her, it kept her laughing. I crossed the street, walking right by them as I entered the laundromat. I grabbed a bag of chips from one of the vending machines, and went into my office to eat them and drink my soda. As I looked at my watch, I had thirty minutes to get to my appointment with the man who owned the other building I was considering. I waited for a few minutes, wondering if Poetry was going to wrap up her conversation. Ten minutes later she did, and came into my office.

"Do you need me to stay or will you be here for the rest of the day?" she asked.

"Why?" I asked, smacking loudly on the chips. "You got somethin' else to do?"

"No. But if you're paying me to be here, it doesn't make sense for you to be here too."

"I'm leavin' in a few to go take care of some things. But, uh, who was ol' boy you was outside talkin' to?"

"That was Anthony. He's home for a while and stopped by to say hello."

"How did he know you were here?"

"I told him. I know you ain't trippin', Prince, and until you come clean about you and your skeletons, you shouldn't have no say-so about who I talk to."

"I don't, but you're the one who said that he played the shit out of you. I can't believe you're runnin' back to a married man. It kind of surprises me, and I didn't think you were that desperate or, to be frank, stupid."

Her hand touched her hip. "Look, he just came to say hello, and you need to watch your mouth calling me desperate and stupid. Besides, ain't nothing going on between us, but if it was, it's none of your business. You showed me that you ain't feeling this, and all I'm here to do is make my money and be gone. "

I stood up, crumbled the chips bag in my hand, and downed the rest of my soda. I tossed the can in a trash can and stood next to Poetry before making my way out. "Don't invite that nigga here again. Meet up with him at your house, and if you pull that shit again, you're goin' to see a side of me that you may not like."

Poetry moved her head back, shocked by my tone. I left before she had anything else to say. Since I'd become her boss, she learned fast to keep her mouth shut. I guessed she didn't want to lose out on any money, and I reminded her, before, that back talk wasn't needed.

I got to my appointment five minutes late. From the outside, the building looked as if it would be big enough, but the inside was too small. The man did his best to get me to sign a lease, as the property he owned had been vacant for some time.

"Come on, dude. I really need to rent this place out. I can take two hundred dollars off the rent and pay the electric bill for you for a year."

Even though that was a good damn deal, I still couldn't see myself downsizing to a place this small. I would only be able to get half of the customers at my current place in here, and would eventually lose money.

"Nah, bro," I said, shaking his hand. "But thanks for your time."

I left, and instead of going back to the laundromat, I stopped to get me some KFC, then went to Mama's house. For whatever reason, I had hoped that one day I would show up and she would be there. Today wasn't my lucky day, and as I checked the rooms, again, nothing had changed. I went into my bedroom and sat on my bed. I fumbled with my nails, then dropped back on the bed and looked at the ceiling. Memories of me and Mama started swirling in my head. I smiled at the good times and shook my head at the bad times. We sure as hell had our ups and downs, but I needed her so badly. I needed to hear her voice, even though she would probably be cussing me out right about now. I smiled from the thought, then sighed from frustrations. I didn't really want to go where I was thinking about

going, but calling on Him, again, seemed like the right
thing to do. I closed my eyes, asking God for His help.

"Please," I said. "I know I haven't done right, but
don't make Mama pay for my mistakes. Bring her back
and take me. I don't know how you go about doin'
things, but every time I come to you with problems,
you never seem to work them out in my favor. Just this
one time, please, come through for me. Amen."

I opened my eyes and sat up on the bed. For the
next few hours, I hung around watching TV, eating
my chicken, and playing video games. It was getting
pretty late, so I locked the door and drove back to the
laundromat. When I got there, several people were inside and one lady was fussing because she had put her
money into the detergent machine and nothing came
out. Since it was after nine o'clock, I figured Poetry
had already left. But one of her responsibilities was to
make sure the detergent and change machines were
filled. When I opened the machine, the whole thing was
almost empty. Mad as hell, I went to my closet, giving
the lady an extra box of detergent for her troubles. I
guessed Poetry had Anthony's dick on her mind, and
she couldn't wait to go see him. The thought truly
pissed me off, and how dare she neglect my business
for a cheating-ass fool?

"Thank you," the lady said, walking away to finish
her laundry. "Oh." She turned around. "The bathroom
needs to be cleaned up. I went in there to use it and
somebody did number two and didn't flush the toilet."

"Appreciate you for lettin' me know. I'll get on it."

I didn't bother to go to the bathroom, as I could already imagine what it looked like. Yet again, that was
one of Poetry's responsibilities that she failed to do. I
called her to see why she hadn't filled the machines like
I told her to, and to question her about the bathroom,

but got no answer. My blood was boiling over, so I got in my car and drove to her house. No sooner had I turned the corner than I saw the blue Saturn from earlier parked where my motorcycle was that day. I couldn't see any lights on inside, and as I reached for the doorknob to open the door, I quickly changed my mind. I wasn't about to get myself caught up into no bullshit about no chick who didn't seem worth it. If she wanted to hook back up with her ex, so damn what? My feelings were a little bruised, but over the years, I had learned how to handle these kinds of setbacks with females. Nothing surprised me about them, so I had to chalk that shit up and move on.

I drove back to the laundromat, and as I sat in my car getting high, I hated what I was feeling inside for Poetry. I regretted that I let my guard down and kicked up some feelings for a chick I really didn't know much about. I kept picturing old boy fucking her and had no one but myself to blame for many missed opportunities. Maybe I should have told her what was going on with me, but then again, that probably wouldn't have mattered. Her legs would still be cocked open right now, being served by her soldier boy. I was so damn jealous, and it surprised me just how jealous I was. Normally, shit like this could roll off my back, but as the night went on, my thoughts of her were sticking with me. I debated going back to her house just to see if her ex had left. I struggled with my thoughts, and by then, my mind was already made up. I was in front of her house, again, seeing that his car was still there. I did a U-turn, then went back home. Eager to tear into something, I went upstairs to Jenay's apartment. But as I approached the door, I could already hear some action going on inside. Sounded like she and her lover were having some fun, and unless I was invited, I didn't want to interrupt.

Not ready to call it a night, I got back in my car and drove around for a while. I asked a few fellas hanging out in front of a bar if they knew G, or where I could find him. Nobody knew nothing. I even drove to East St. Louis, looking around and trying to see if I could find him. No luck. To waste more time, I pulled out my fake ID and went to the casino. Played several hands on the blackjack tables and threw money into a slot machine that gave me an eight-hundred-dollar payout. By the time I got done and cashed in my tickets, it was almost six o'clock in the morning. The casino was about to close for a few hours. With fat pockets, I drove back home, slept for three hours, then went to the laundromat to see if Poetry had opened up at eight like she was supposed to.

I pushed the door open, seeing her in the back, mopping the floor. At least four customers were already inside washing.

"Why in the fuck didn't you put any detergent in the machines like I told you to?" I shouted at her. "And the bathroom in there is a damn mess! I guess yo' ass didn't have time, and since you ain't got time to do shit like I asked you to do, yo' ass fired! Get the fuck out. I'll mail your check to you at the end of the week!"

Poetry's mouth dropped open and she rushed to my office with the mop in her hand. She pointed it at me as rage covered her face. "For your information, Negro, I couldn't open the damn machine after you left because you had the keys on you! I called you several times, but you did not answer. I just got done cleaning up that nasty-ass bathroom and somebody must have messed it up after I left, because before then it was sparkling clean!" She let go of the mop and it hit the floor. "As for this job, you can shove it up your ass, especially if you think you're going to come in here talking to me like that. Just who in the hell do you think you are? 'Cause to me, you ain't shit!"

Poetry was getting ready to exit, but I jumped up and closed the door. I held it shut with my hand so she wouldn't leave. My voice lowered, as what she said could have been possible. I'd left my phone in the car while I was at Mama's house, and while I was at the casino. The keys, indeed, were in my pocket all along. My mind was so fucked up that I forgot.

"Look, I apologize for goin' off on you like that and I'm sorry. I'm just on edge right now and a lot of shit—"

"What you got going on, Prince? Tell me. I've been waiting to hear your excuse for a very long time. I get so tired of you saying the same old thing over and over without explaining yourself."

I let go of the door and put my hands in my pockets. "What did you do last night?" I asked.

Poetry folded her arms. "None of your business. Now, I asked you a question and I want some answers. And just so you know, I'm not telling you nothing until you come clean with me."

"You were with *him* last night, weren't you?"

"And you were with *her* last night, weren't you? Tell me, Prince, who is she? Who got your damn brain so twisted that you can't even recognize a decent woman when you see one?"

"Is that what you're callin' yourself these days? A decent woman don't go around fuckin' married men. Tricks and hoes do, and from what I see, you're wearin' your title pretty well."

Poetry reached out and slapped the shit out of me. Now, if there ever came a time that I would put my hands on a female, this was it. I lunged forward and shoved her against my desk. I grabbed her by her neck and squeezed it. She scratched at my hand, causing me to snatch it away. I darted my finger at her with a heaving chest. "Do you really want to know what the fuck is up with me, you stupid-ass girl? I'll tell you what! I don't take no shit from nobody and I will kill any motherfucka who crosses me and puts their hands on me. Been there, done that! That other woman you keep talkin' about is my damn mother! She's been missin' for almost two months and I don't know where the fuck she is! So I don't have time for a bunch of bullshit right now, especially when I don't know if she's dead or alive!"

I turned around, not wanting Poetry to see my emotions. She touched my back, but I shrugged her off me. Her voice softened. "I'm so sorry, Prince, and had I known—"

I quickly turned around. "Had you known, you would have still been fuckin' with me about why I couldn't spend my time on no damn relationship. That's all some of y'all chicks want is for somebody to take care of y'all and give y'all some dick. I hope you got it in last night, that way you can stop sweatin' the fuck out of me!"

Poetry glared at me, as I seemed to have lost it. She remained calmed, though, and that really surprised me. "Your words sting, but I have never been one to wait around for nobody to do anything for me. I couldn't care less about some dick, and for your information, nothing happened between me and Anthony last night."

I stepped up face-to-face with her. "Really now? Then, why was he at your damn house all night? Don't lie, Poetry, because I saw his car parked out there all night."

"Are you stalking me or something? Look, dude," she said, pushing me away from her, "I am out of here. You got some serious issues. I just told you that I didn't do anything with him."

She charged toward the door, but I pushed her against my desk again. I hit the light switch and sniffed out her perfume in the dark. I pressed my body against hers, then held her face in my hands. My voice was calm, as I sought out a legitimate answer to my question. "If you didn't do anything with him, then why was his car outside of your house all night? Just answer that for me, please."

"He met me at my house after work, Prince. We talked outside for about thirty minutes, and when he got in his car, it wouldn't start. I took him to his mother's house, and he left his car at my house all night. When I left this morning, it was still there. I don't know when he's going to get somebody to come pick it up, and that is the truth."

"You still want to get with that fool or what? I saw the way you looked at him yesterday, Poetry, and that look in your eyes said somethin' was there."

"No," she said, removing my sweaty hands from her face. "I was being nice and the only person I'm interested in right now is you. I'm sorry about what you've been going through, and if I can do anything to help you find your mother, let me know. Don't shut me out. Just give me a chance to be there for you, okay?"

Poetry held my waist and as we started to kiss, her lips put me at ease. I moved my mouth away from her lips and sucked her neck. "I'm no good, baby. I'm tellin' you now that I've done a lot of shit in my life that I'm not proud of."

"Haven't we all," she said. She pulled my shirt over my head and started to unbutton my shorts. Her one-piece stretch dress was easy access, and as I pulled it over her head, I felt for her G-string panties and pulled them down. The aroma of her peach-smelling body infused the tiny room, exciting me even more. I dropped my shorts to my ankles and stepped out of them. Poetry sat up on my cluttered desk, and when something hit the floor, she laughed. "Oops," she said, then wrapped her legs around me and massaged my bare ass. I wanted to taste her so badly, but my dick was already moving in the direction of her heat. I held the tip of my head, circling her moist hole, then easing myself inside. Poetry rested back on her elbows, knocking even more things off my desk. I held her legs apart, and dug myself inside of her like I was digging for precious gold. The sounds of her juices stirring filled the room and so did her delicate moans.

"I knew this dick was going to feel good," she said in a whisper. "Damn, Prince, this shit feels too good."

I kept quiet, but the sex felt nice to me too. I ground tough on her insides, stretching her tight pussy even wider. And when my pace picked up, Poetry leaned forward and held on to my neck. Our bodies slapped against each other as she worked the lower part of her body like a pro. I gave her long strokes, deep strokes that wet my shaft even more. Her whole body was trembling and I could feel her legs shaking in my arms. I leaned in to wet her lips with my saliva, then dropped my head to suck her nipples. They were tiny, but as I teased them, she was on fire.

"Stooooop," she said, pushing me back. "I don't want to come yet."

Poetry got down from my desk and when she turned around, I stood behind her. I pressed myself against her, then beat my dick against her ass to keep it hard. She leaned over my desk, spreading her legs even wider. My muscle slipped back into her wetness, and as I held her tiny waist from behind, I tore it up. The loud slaps against her ass sounded off in the room and my dick was one happy motherfucka. Poetry was working her hips and ass well, throwing it back and keeping it at a rhythm that had me high.

"Ssssss, shit!" I yelled. She was fucking me well. I had to stop for a second to regroup, as the hot lava oozing from her pussy was no joke. I pulled out of her and squatted to fill my belly with her cream. And by the time I was finished, her body lay straight on my desk like a flying airplane. She was tense all over and screamed as I licked along her furrows and tried to swallow her clit.

"Oh, my, daaaamn, Prince! Stop, baby, ooooo, stoooop!"

My tongue was deep within her. It traveled from one hole to the other, and as Poetry reached her climax, she was spent. She could barely stand up. I secured her in my arms, then moved over to my chair. She straddled my lap, resting her arms on my shoulders.

"I surely didn't want our first time together to be in a place like this. I know those people out there can hear us and you should be ashamed of yourself for doing that to me," she said.

"We can always turn the lights back on and call it a wrap. But I've been holdin' this nut, and when I bust it, yo' ass is gon' be somewhere in la la land."

Poetry was determined to *bring* out the best in me. She lifted herself, then carefully eased down on my dick. At first, she rode me slow, then she arched her back and sped up the pace. My hands touched her slimming curves from her back, to her perfect waist, then to her smooth ass. I lifted it and helped her ride me to the rhythm of my satisfaction. She was so good at what she was doing, and when she turned around to ride me backward, my head dropped back in the chair.

I dropped my arms by my side and my toes tightened and curled.

"Ride that motherfucka, ma," I said, moving fast with her, about to break the squeaking chair. She proceeded to go faster and that's when my body went limp, feeling like every ounce of semen in me rushed out. I grabbed Poetry from behind, squeezing her tightly in my arms. She kept teasing me, and kept on moving.

"Don't do that shit," I said. My dick was so sensitive from the beating it had taken, but it was a beating that caused for no retaliation. Well, in a good way, of course.

Poetry got up and flipped on the lights. She spotted her dress on the floor and pulled it over her head. I put on my shorts, and as we were now able to look each other in the eyes, all we could do was smile.

"I need a shower," she said. "Either I can go home or go upstairs to your apartment."

"I need a shower too, so we can shower together. That's if you want to."

Poetry shrugged and opened the door. "Why not?" she said and walked out. I followed and every single eye in the place was on us. More people had come in, and Poetry looked embarrassed as hell. I wasn't at all, and as I made my way upstairs, she messed around in the laundromat, pretending as if she had work to do. Shortly thereafter, she knocked on my door and joined me in the shower. I felt so at ease with her, and at this point, I regretted not letting her into my life sooner.

# Chapter Eleven

## Eyes Wide Open . . .

Poetry and me had been hanging tight. I'd gotten a chance to meet her grandmother, and had introduced her to Nate. He seemed to really like her, and had nothing but good things to say about her when she wasn't in our presence. It made me feel as if I'd made the right choice this time around, and to be honest, I kind of dug having a girlfriend. Hadn't had one I could call my own for a very long time, and even though Nadine and me had gotten pretty cool, I always saw her as just my baby's mama.

Other than that, I wished like hell that Mama could meet Poetry. I knew she'd have some gripes about her, but eventually, like me, Mama would see all of the good things about her that I liked so much. I still hadn't given up on my search for her, and almost every single day I did drive-bys to see if G or any of his partners had been hanging around. It was as if he had fallen off the earth, and when I talked to Raylo, he said the same thing. I guess he'd gotten to a point where he'd given up, because his phone calls to let me know what was going on were limited. We barely talked to each other these days, but when I stopped by Mama's house, sometimes he was there, many times he wasn't.

Meanwhile, Poetry was doing her best to keep my mind off my troubles. I spilled my guts to her, telling her about everything that had happened with Romeo getting caught up, on down to me killing my father. Told her about Nadine being shot up, and about the fools I had to do away with who were responsible. She understood me better than anyone, and nothing that I said to her made her fearful or leery about being with me. I guess she understood so well because Poetry had been through some shit too. Her mother had her on the stroll with her at twelve years old. She was raped and got pregnant by the man who raped her. She had an abortion, but was raped again by her uncle who abused her as well. She wound up stabbing him one day, and was put in juvenile for a while. All she did in there was fight, and once she was let go, she went back to live with her grandmother. After finding out that her son raped Poetry, her grandmother made him leave, and ever since then, it had been about the two of them, taking care of each other.

That was until Anthony came on the scene. All they did was fight each other, and Poetry told me about the many black eyes he'd given her. She stressed how possessive he was, but when all was said and done, she still loved him. He was the one to call it quits, and the reason that he was back was because his marriage had failed and he wanted Poetry back. I took her word that she wanted nothing to do with him, and after all that she'd been through with him, I assumed he was history.

Nate gave me some tickets to a Rams football game, so I invited my girl to go with me. There weren't too many places I'd go without her, as we had gotten very close over the last month. So close that I completely ignored Jenay when I saw her, and even though Francine was already history, I ignored her too. It was all about Poetry and I had it really bad for her.

Since it was chilly outside, we wore jackets and jeans to stay warm. I drove to the Edward Jones Dome to see the game, and as usual, Poetry complained about my driving.

"One day, you gon' hurt somebody driving this car as fast as you do. I'm surprised that you haven't gotten any tickets. Don't you worry about the police pulling you over?"

"Nope, because I'm good at watchin' my surroundings. I can spot a police car a mile away. I know which areas are hot, and which ones are not. And if I do get pulled over, I'll man up and pay my ticket. No problem there."

"Well, you won't have to man up if you slow down. I can't believe you got all this precious cargo over here, and you won't even do what's necessary to protect me."

"I'll always protect you. You don't have to worry about that at all."

Poetry noticed that I had gotten quiet after my comment to her. She knew I was worried about something happening to her, especially since we'd been spending so much time together. "Get that out your head, Prince. I know you got me and I know your mama is still on your mind. But what you gon' do, baby? You still go to her house, and I know it hurts you like hell to go there. You can't let it sit like that, can you? What you plan on doing with her house, especially if she never comes back?"

I shrugged. "I don't know. I have been thinkin' about what to do with her house, and that fool Raylo ain't barely there anymore. It's just sittin' and I don't want nobody to break in and start stealin' shit. Maybe I'll put some of her things in storage."

Poetry reached over and rubbed the back of my head. "I'll help you get some of her things together. Whenever you're ready, let me know."

I nodded, and just to mess with Poetry, I sped off the highway and into the parking garage to park my car. She fussed, but I didn't care. It gave me an opportunity to kiss and make up with her, and I did so on the elevator as it went down.

"Stop poutin' and give me some of those sexy lips," I teased. She puckered, but bit my lip when I leaned in. I tried to pull away, but she held on to my lips with her teeth. "Ooouch! That shit hurt, ma!" I felt my lip for blood, and this time, I was pouting. She laughed, then kissed me the right way.

"Awww, Boo, I'm sorry. I'll make it up to you later and I promise to put in overtime."

"I hope so," I said, getting off the elevator. "You've been gettin' yours lately and leavin' my ass hangin'. You need to put in double overtime or maybe triple."

Poetry stopped and put her hand on her hip. "Don't even go there, Prince. If my calculations are correct, you busted three nuts the last time we were together."

"Three times! Stop yo' lyin', Poetry. I only came once and that was yo' ass on top of that washing machine, actin' a fool. I told you I was gon' make you eat your words about calling my dick pint sized."

"I did not call your dick pint sized. I just said it was little to hurt your feelings. I know better, now, and being on top of that washing machine was fun, wasn't it? Especially when it started spinning. You probably thought it was me going overboard but the machine did most of the work."

"Bullshit," I said, laughing. "It may have helped you move in circles, but the work needs to be credited to me. I made you come, not the washing machine."

This time, Poetry laughed. "Okay. I'll give credit where credit is due, but if I have to start putting in more overtime, you gon' have to pay me. Shoot!"

I got behind Poetry and wrapped my arms around her. I kissed her cheek and licked inside of her ear. "You know you can have anything you want. You're too damn good to me and I promise to always be good to you too."

Poetry turned around to give me a long, wet kiss. I was trying my best not to fall for her, but it was too late. I was prepared to do anything in the world for her, but I wasn't sure that she knew how I felt. For whatever reason, I kept my feelings to myself. I wanted to be sure, because some things were too good to be true.

We walked down the street holding hands, but before we got to the Dome, I saw a bunch of old-school cars lined up that caught my attention. Several older men were driving the cars, and they were surrounded by a gang of people admiring them. I couldn't help but admire the cars too, but when I saw Raylo behind the wheel of Ernie's 1965 Lincoln, I was surprised. I knew he hadn't gone back to get his car that night, and I wondered how in the hell he'd gotten it. I started to go over to him and ask, but something told me not to. Instead, I slowed my pace, stopping Poetry as we neared the door.

"Say, if you don't mind, I need to go check out something real quick. We may not make it to the game and I hope you ain't mad at me."

"I'm not a big football fan, but what do you need to do?"

I gave Poetry my keys and pointed to the corner. "Do me a favor and go get my car. I'ma be right there on that corner, so pick me up right there."

She put her hand on her hip and sighed. "Prince, what are you up to?"

"I'll tell you in a minute. Just go do what I asked you to. Please."

Poetry took my keys and headed to the parking garage. I ran across the street, getting a closer look at all of the other men and Raylo in their cars. It wasn't the men who actually caught my attention, but more so the women. I remembered the white chick who was at G's place that day, Peaches. She was in the car with another one of the men, and I found that to be quite odd. Then, another thing came to mind. G mentioned what we had done to Ernie. How in the hell did he know, if it was just me and Raylo there doing our thing? There was a possibility that we'd been followed, but at that moment, something about the whole thing didn't feel right to me. As I continued to look on, I saw Poetry coming with my car. She pulled up to the curb and I got inside.

"Let's get out of here," I said. She drove off, and kept looking suspiciously at me.

"So, are you going to tell me what's going on?" she asked.

"Baby, I think I've been set the fuck up. Big . . . big time."

"Set up by who?"

"By Raylo. I think he's the one who did somethin' to my mother and had me runnin' around like crazy tryin' to find her."

"Didn't you say they'd been together for years? You said he loved her. Why would he set you up? What could he possibly have to gain?"

"Money. That nigga asked me for some money right before Mama disappeared. I wouldn't give it to him, and the next thing I know, she's missin'. But what I don't understand is why he would want me to kill his friend to get some money when he stood to gain money from G, if they were in this together all along?"

Poetry slammed on the brakes and pulled the car over. "Wait. You just confused the hell out of me. Who is G and who were you supposed to kill?"

I hadn't gotten into details with Poetry about what I'd done to Ernie, or about my issues with G. I explained to Poetry that I suspected Raylo saw an opportunity to kill Ernie and get some of his money and cars because he'd been hating, not because he was trying to help me. Either way, Poetry seemed mad. "I can't believe y'all did that man like that. That was cold, Prince, and you shouldn't have ever gone to his house. I've never met Raylo, but please keep me away from his ass. He seems too vicious for me, and I hope to God you are done with all of this mess. Your eyes say you're not, Prince, and I'ma be so mad at you if you ever think about going after those fools. They will kill you and it's best that you leave well enough alone."

"So, I'm just supposed to sit back and be made a fool of? Is that what you're sayin'? What about my Mama? What if Raylo was the one who did somethin' to her?"

"Call the police, Prince. Let them deal with it. This may be too much for you to handle and I don't want you to keep runnin' around here killin' people because they pissed you off."

"Pissed me off!" I shouted and cocked my head back. "I don't kill people for pissin' me off, and if that was the case, you'd be dead. I deal with those who fuck with me to the point where it affects me and those around me. I'm not some trigger-happy nigga tryin' to get a reputation or a badge for doin' the unthinkable. You need to come better than that and check yourself for bein' incorrect."

"No, you need to calm yourself down and listen to what I'm trying to tell you. I'm not saying that you shouldn't be upset if someone did something to your mother. What I'm saying is you are not above the law. Stop putting the law into your own hands, and put it into the hands of those who it belongs with. If you wind up dead or in jail, how you gon' protect the ones you say you care about? I know you wouldn't be able to do a damn thing for me in jail, and all I'm doing is trying to talk some sense into you before it's too late."

"We need to squash this conversation right now. All I'm gon' say to you is if I find out Raylo set me up, and my mama is dead, I'ma deal with him myself. I'll go to jail for makin' sure justice is served for her and that's just tellin' you straight like it is. Take it or leave it."

Poetry sat silent for a while, tapping the steering wheel with her fingers and looking straight ahead. "And what about me, Prince? What am I supposed to do if you go to jail? No matter what, you still gotta be here for me, too, don't you? Or have I been fooling myself, thinking that I've found the man of my dreams? Don't you know that I've fallen in love with you? I don't want to lose you this soon. I think we got something special that can go a long, long way. Have I been wrong, Prince? Please tell me that I haven't been wrong about us. I'm not in this by myself, am I?"

I didn't respond, as I really didn't have time for no soap opera bullshit Poetry was spilling right now. No, she wasn't wrong about us, but it was hard to explain that I had to deal with this situation about my mother, no matter what. "No matter what I say to you, it's not gon' sit right with you. So I'ma cut this conversation short, so we can keep it movin' down the highway."

Poetry didn't budge. "So, I guess I have been wrong about us. This was all about you getting some pussy. I can't be mad at you because it's what you stressed from the beginning. You don't give a damn about me, Prince, and if you did, you wouldn't sit there and say what you just did. Either way, it looks as if I'm going to be left without, so we may as well call it quits right now."

She opened the car door and got out. Cars were zooming by us, and I couldn't believe we were parked near the highway, dealing with this dumbass shit right now. I got out and slammed my door.

"Will you get back in the damn car and quit trippin'!" I yelled.

Poetry kept on walking, ignoring me. I ran up from behind her, and yanked her arm. "Don't touch me!" she shouted. "Why don't you leave me the fuck alone and go kill some damn body."

"I'ma kill yo' ass if you don't get yo' shit together. Now, stop fuckin' with me, Poetry, and get back in the car!"

"Like hell! I don't take threats like that too lightly and, fool, you'd better think twice . . ."

As she rambled on, I picked her up by her legs and threw her over my shoulder. She kicked and tried to make me lose my balance, but it didn't work. I opened the car door, and dropped her on the front seat. I then kneeled down beside her, doing my best to calm the situation that I seriously didn't have time for. "Look, you ain't wastin' your time, all right? I'm feelin' some-thin' good inside too, and if this was all about some pussy, you know I would've been gone. Just be patient with me on this. I'm still tryin' to deal with the loss of my mama, and it's normal for me to say what I would do to somebody under the circumstances. If it were you, you'd probably be threatin' to kill somebody too. I don't know what I would really do, but I do know that I need you right now. You've helped me get through this and I ain't never felt for nobody in my life how I feel about you. I would never hurt you and I'm sorry for sayin' that bullshit to you. I said it out of anger and I was wrong for goin' there."

Poetry sat silent for a while, then put her legs inside of
the car and let me close the door. I got in on the driver's
side, and drove us straight to Nate's apartment. I really
needed his advice about what I suspected was going on
with Raylo, but when I sat at his kitchen table and told
him, I was surprised by his response. He touched my
shoulder and recited Romans 12:19:

*Do not take revenge, my friend, but leave room for
God's wrath, for it is written: "It's mine to avenge, I
will repay."*

"I get all of that," I said to Nate. "But God don't be
answerin' my prayers. He ain't got no love for a nigga
like me."

Poetry covered her mouth, and mumbled, "I can't believe you said that! Have I fallen in love with the devil?
Are you crazy, Prince? After all you told me that you've
been through, and you're still alive and not behind bars!
How can you doubt that He been looking out for you?
He could have given up on you a long time ago. You'd
better recognize and pray for forgiveness, especially for
saying something so stupid like that!"

"I'm afraid I have to agree with Poetry," Nate said.
"You have a lot to learn, Prince, but I thought you were
much smarter than that. Stop takin' the bad from your
situations and look at all the good. From what I see,
you got your own businesses, you ain't wantin' for
much, you got a smart and fine young lady in your corner, and you're alive. What more do you want?"

"I know that's right," Poetry said, adding her two
cents and snapping her fingers in the air. "Some people
are so ungrateful, and I'm surprised at you, Prince.
What more do you want?"

I paused before responding, then looked at Poetry
and Nate both. "I want to see my mother. If something
has happened to her, I want the people who hurt her to
be dealt with."

"Keep on praying for that to happen," Nate said. "But don't go gettin' ahead of God, as you'll fuck yourself. Lay low, Prince, and eventually this situation will work itself out."

"If you say so," I said, standing to leave and stretching. Didn't get much help from Nate, and I should have known that he would preach to me about staying on the right track.

"In due time," Nate said again while walking us to the door. "It will all work out."

I seriously didn't know how it would work out, but as me and Poetry drove to Mama's house, I was hopeful that a turning point was coming soon. Seeing Raylo had my mind going a mile a minute and I had a feeling that things were about to get ugly. I decided to gather some of Mama's important things, just in case somebody started snooping around and stealing her stuff. Poetry had never been to Mama's house before, and I was glad to show her where I'd grown up. I showed her around our tiny house, and when I showed her my room, she laughed.

"You know what? I pictured your room looking like this. I didn't think it would be this clean, but I figured you had trophies on your shelves, pictures of scantily dressed women on your walls, and a whole lot of video games."

"Yep," I said, sitting on my bed. "My room has been like this for years. The only reason it's this clean is because of my mama. She used to clean it up for me all the time, and when I tell you I used to fuck somethin' up, I mean I really used to mess somethin' up. She'd come in, spraying Lysol and goin' the fuck off on me. I had some good times in this room and you have no idea how it used to go down in here."

"Oh, I can only imagine," Poetry said, sitting next to me. "I know your son was conceived in this room, and I assume all those broads you screwed in high school had the time of their lives in here, too. Do you ever think about what if you had pursued your football career? I saw many of the newspaper articles about you, and with all of these trophies, don't you think you could have seriously made it?"

"Possibly, but I didn't really have a passion for playin' football. I was damn good, but I was doin' it more so for the attention. It could've been my way out, but who knows. Can't look back on that shit now 'cause those days are long gone."

I lay back on the bed and Poetry rested her head on my chest. "What about your sons, Prince? When are you going to see what's up with them? I know Nadine's mom has one of your sons, but you haven't put forth much effort to find him. Your other son still lives in St. Louis, don't he? Why don't you try to make a connection with him? I'm just saying this to you because every child needs their father. These boys don't need to be growing up without, and we both know how not having our daddies around has affected us. Don't let the cycle continue with you, and do what you can to stop it. I'm saying all of this to say that if we stay together, I can never have your kids. The second time I was raped and got pregnant, I did something to myself that messed me up forever. I don't have to tell you what it was, but it was illegal and my insides haven't been the same since."

I kissed Poetry's forehead, thanking her for being honest with me. "I'll deal with the situation with my sons when I can. I promise."

Poetry got off the bed and went to my computer desk. She turned on my computer, then looked at me. "What's Monesha's last name?"

"Thompson," I said. She typed in something, and a few minutes later, she turned to me again.

"Voilà. Thank God for Facebook, huh? Do you know if she goes to SLU and if she went to West High School? I see some cheerleading pictures out here and some baby pics, too. Come look and see if this is her."

I got off the bed slightly irritated that Poetry was doing this, but I knew how she was. I looked at the picture and it was definitely Monesha. I also looked at the boy who was in some of the pictures with her and with her parents. I didn't think he looked like me, but Poetry said he kind of did.

"Just a little, but you can never be too sure. Let's send her a message and see if she responds."

"Come on, ma. I don't want to do all of that right now. Let's just lie back down and chill."

"No, Prince. Let's get this over with so you will know. Besides, you owe it to your son; that's if he's yours."

I shook my head and watched as Poetry sent Monesha a detailed e-mail from me, asking if the little boy was mine. She stressed that I wanted to see him and was willing to do my part, *if* I was his father. She asked Monesha to get back to me soon through e-mail, or by phone. After typing my cell phone number, Poetry hit the send button.

"There," she said, swiping her hands together. "All done and now we wait."

I fell back on the bed and Poetry crawled over me. "I thought we came here to pack up some of your mother's things. It's getting late and I'm getting tired. Do you want to stay the night here, or come back tomorrow?"

"Let's stay. I'll gather some things in the mornin', then we can go."

Poetry got underneath the covers with me, and as she talked my ears off, I finally fell asleep. I dreamed that God had answered my prayers, and in my dream, He had let me know exactly where Mama was. As expected, it wasn't good and I jumped up from my sleep in a sweat. I stared at the wall in front of me, fearing to close my eyes again.

# Chapter Twelve

## The Truth Will Set No One Free

Poetry was still at Mama's house asleep. I had gone to McDonald's to get us some breakfast, and when I got back, I woke her up. The dream I'd had weighed heavily on my mind, and something about today didn't feel right to me at all.

"What time is it?" she asked while stretching her arms. "I slept so good last night and was out like a light."

"It's a little after eight. My bed may be small, but it is comfortable. I already called Nate to ask him to open the laundromat for me, but once we get done here, I need to go check on a few things over there."

Poetry nodded and got off the bed. She headed for the bathroom. "I know you don't have any extra toothbrushes around here, do you? And where can I find a face towel?"

I opened a linen closet, giving her a face towel. "As for a toothbrush, you may have to use your finger. Don't have any extra ones, unless you care to use mine."

"Ughhh, that's nasty. My finger will work just fine."

She went into the bathroom and closed the door behind her. I headed for the kitchen, and sat at the table to eat my hotcakes and sausage. When Poetry came into the kitchen, she sat on my lap and puckered for a kiss.

"That was quick," I said. "Did you get them teeth and that tongue good?"

She squeezed my cheeks together with her hand. "Nah, but you don't care."

We kissed and she was so damn right. I didn't care and the excitement I always felt inside during our intimate moments like these made me smile.

Poetry wrapped one of her arms around my neck and started feeding me the pancakes. I opened my mouth and chewed. "What do you be thinking about all the time, Prince? Like when you just smiled, what was on your mind? You rarely show your emotions and I be so puzzled when I see you spaced out and in deep thought."

I shrugged, as I was never one to wear my emotions on my sleeve "I be thinkin' about us a lot. About how happy I am to have you, more than anything."

Poetry kissed my cheek then stood up. She playfully twisted her hips and jumped around. "Prince got a girl-friend, Prince got a girlfriend . . . finally, y'all, Prince got a girlfriend!"

I grabbed her arm, pulling her back on my lap. "You silly," I said, blushing. "My girlfriend better hurry up and eat before she get left."

Poetry quickly put the sausage in her mouth, then took a bite of one of the pancakes. "Ooooo, I almost forgot," she said, jumping up again. "I need to go check the computer to see if Monesha responded."

She ran off to my room before I could say anything. I guess I wasn't as hyped as she was, so I stayed at the table, finishing my food.

Poetry didn't come back until about ten minutes later. She stood in the doorway and cleared her throat. I looked in her direction, but she didn't say anything. All she did was motion her finger for me to come to her.

I guess I didn't move fast enough and that's when she said, "Come here. You need to read this."

I got up from the table and followed her into my room. I pulled my chair back and started reading Monesha's response to the e-mail Poetry had sent on my behalf.

Prince "Pretty Boy" Perkins, it's always good hearing from you and what a surprise. There isn't a day that goes by where I don't think about you and all of the fun we had during high school. I never got a chance to apologize to you about giving you a STD, but now is my chance. I'm sorry, and I know what I'd done angered you. I also know you spoke to my father about my baby, and as I sat there that day, listening to him go off on you about handling your responsibilities as a father, I could have killed myself. I didn't have the guts to tell him that I'd had sex with three boys in one week, and didn't really know who the father was at the time. I chose you because I liked you and I knew you'd be making big dollars some day. Forgive me, again, for being so confused, but I started going to church and decided to get my life on the right track. After all, I do have a beautiful son who changed my life in so many ways. That son, however, is not yours and he has a great relationship with his biological father. I regret stressing you with this situation and my hope is that it has not hindered your life in any way. Thanks for the e-mail, Street Soldier, and let me know if you ever have time to do lunch with a friend.

I took a deep breath, relieved in so many ways. Something that wracked my brain was now behind me, and all I could do was look at Poetry and thank her for having the courage when I didn't. "Give me a hug," I said to her.

She stepped forward while I sat in the chair and eased my arms around her waist. She kissed the top of my head, then backed up. "You better not go have lunch with her and, when I delete this e-mail, no need to reach out to her again, right?"

"None. Even though she's lookin' damn good, I'ma keep my hormones intact."

Poetry pulled me up from the chair. "Uh, she's cute, but sista girl ain't got nothing on me. Now, let's get started so we can get back to your apartment and release some of the energy we didn't get a chance to release last night. Besides, I'm kind of feeling the washing machine thingy again. We can put an OUT TO LUNCH sign on the door and close the blinds."

"You know I'm always down with that, so let's get moving."

As Poetry cleaned off the kitchen table and threw the McDonald's bags in the trash, I went into Mama's room. I opened her drawers, pulling out some of her jewelry that was still there. I was surprised Raylo's punk ass hadn't taken any of her things to the pawn shop, and my suspicions about him were growing by the minute. I stood for a moment in a trance about my next move. Poetry didn't have to know what my intentions were, and even though I appreciated the advice Nate had given me, I guessed neither of them really knew me too well. I had it all planned out in my head. I was going to some of Raylo's hangouts today to go find him. I was going to lay it all on the line for him, and if he looked me in the eyes and admitted to doing something to Mama, no doubt about it, I was going to kill him. Jail time or not, he had to be dealt with.

Poetry knocked on the door to get my attention, snapping me out of my thoughts. "What did you say?" I asked.

"I said, where is the trash dumpster at? I need to go throw this trash away. When I come back, I'm going to help you get a move on it. You've been standing there for several minutes and haven't done much. What's on your mind?"

"Nothing much."

I looked out the window in front of me, seeing the trash can we used to take our trash to the dumpster in an alley. The trash can was next to our garage that was barely still standing. "Take it out to the blue trash can out back. Be careful 'cause the grass is pretty high. I don't want no snakes to jump out and bite that ass."

"Don't play. Ain't no snakes in the hood, and if there is one back there, you will never have to worry about me coming over here again."

Poetry took the trash out and I watched through the window as she tiptoed over the tall grass and made her way to the trash can. Her face was twisted and she frowned as she opened the can and dumped the bag into it. She hurried back inside and I heard her wash her hands in the kitchen. When she came back to my mama's room, she was fanning her nose.

"It really, really stinks back there. I almost threw the hell up and somebody needs to take that nasty trash to the dumpster."

"Was it that much in there? I didn't think it was a lot of trash in there."

"It was only a small bag in there, but that shit stinks. Smells like something died back there."

As soon as those words left Poetry's mouth, my head snapped to the side. "What did you say?" I asked her.

"I said, it smells like something di . . ." She paused. "No, not that kind of smell, Prince. It was a smell like . . . like, I don't know."

I rushed past Poetry, making my way through the backyard and to the trash can. Poetry called after me, but kept her distance. I could already smell the strong stench in the air and it was the same smell, but even worse, that I had smelled each time I came to Mama's house. Raylo claimed it was the next door neighbor's barbecue, but I should have known that no barbecue that I had eaten had ever smelled like that. I raised the lid on the trash can, and whatever the awful smell was, it damn near burned my nose. I removed the trash bag Poetry had put inside, and that's when I saw the other bag. Inside was a bunch of dirty papers, and underneath that were two dead rabbits that somebody had put into the can. Maggots and flies were all over them and I hurried to close the can to take it to the big dumpster in the alley. Poetry yelled from afar, "What is it?"

"Dead rabbits," I said as we both sighed from relief. "I'm gon' take the trash can to the dumpster. I'll be right back."

I rolled the trash can down the alley, then dumped it into the big dumpster. It still had a horrible-ass smell, and I couldn't believe that the trash can had permeated the air as it had. I looked for some strong cleaners when I got back to the house, but the only things I found were some bleach and Pine-Sol. For now, it had to do. I put on some rubber gloves, and Poetry went outside with me. She watched as I scrubbed the trash can, still frowning from the smell. At this point, she was covering her mouth.

"I'm sorry," she said, coughing. "But it still stinks out here. Hurry up, Prince, so we can go inside."

I hurried to wash the can and couldn't agree with Poetry more. The smell was still in the air, and as we made our way toward the house, something triggered.

I turned and looked at the garage. "Go inside," I said to Poetry. "I'll be there in a minute."

Poetry followed the direction of my eyes, looking at the garage too. "Ma . . . maybe you should call the police, Prince. I don't have a good feeling about this."

Neither did I. My stomach was turned in knots and the way my heart was racing, I didn't like what I was feeling. I slowly walked to the garage, and when I lifted the door, I almost fell backward from the horrible stench that was coming from inside. Mama kept my grandfather's old beat-up Chevy inside that she could never get to work. Rust was all over it, and the garage was cluttered with items my mother had kept of her parents when they died. I lifted my shirt to cover my nose that was burning. I assumed Poetry had already run inside, and when I noticed part of a plastic bag sticking out of the trunk, I backed away. I blinked the water from my eyes, so afraid to open the trunk to see what was inside. The smell was already a giveaway, but I staggered backward as my gaze at the trunk kept me in a trance. Poetry snapped me out of it when she grabbed my arm.

"Prince, please call the police. Let's go inside, baby, okay?"

I backed up, still staring at the trunk. I had a strong feeling about what was inside, and my whole body was weakening by the minute. I staggered inside of the house and dropped back on the couch. Poetry was saying something to me, but I was completely zoned out. I reached for my cell phone in my pocket and called Nate. "Would you do me a favor?" I said softly.

"Sure, man, what's up?"

"Would you make your way to my mama's house as quickly as you can?"

"Uh, sure. Is everything all right?"

"No. Don't think so."

"Let me close up the store. I'll be there as soon as I can."

I hung up and sat like a mannequin, as I was so afraid to face my biggest fear. Mama was dead, killed by the hands of a man who had destroyed our lives and claimed to love her. This wasn't how it was supposed to be, was it? A slow tear rolled down my face, and I regretted that I hadn't dealt with this situation between Mama and Raylo a long time ago. As her son, I could have done something. I should have been man enough to put some fear in Raylo, so he would stop putting his hands on Mama. I felt as if I had let her down. He viewed me as a punk who would never do anything, and those were the exact words he'd said to me after we got back from Ernie's house that day. Now, more than ever, I was determined to show him what was really up with me. And this time, the pleasure would be all mine.

As I sat zoned out and making plans in my head, I could no longer make out anything Poetry was saying to me. Her voice was so loud, and I wasn't trying to hear it. I leaned forward and dropped my face in my hands. "Please!" I screamed. "Shut the fuck up! Damn!" Silence fell over the room.

When Nate showed up, I reached out to give him the keys to the trunk. "Do me a huge favor and check to see what's up with that plastic bag in the trunk of that car in the garage. I can't do it, Nate, and I'm afraid it may be . . ."

Nate snatched the keys from me. "I understand. I'll be right back."

I didn't want to see Mama dead and stuffed into a plastic bag, but the visual in my head was already there. It took awhile for Nate to return, and when he came back inside, I lifted my head to look at him come through the door. Our eyes connected and his stare, as well as blank expression, told me everything I needed to know. He used his shirt to wipe the sheen of sweat from his forehead then two words left his mouth. "I'm sorry."

I closed my eyes, and as I leaned forward again I could barely catch my breath. Tears streamed down my face and my body shook from my staggering cries. A puddle of thick snot and tears formed on the floor down below, as I couldn't even raise my head to look at Poetry, whose cries I could hear as well. Nate rubbed my shoulders, then said he was calling the police. I hated for him to do that, but didn't really have a choice. Within the hour, the police swarmed in, asking a million and one questions. The coroners came, and news reporters were all outside of Mama's house. About ten police officers were inside, three of whom were trying to talk to me. I sat stone faced, saying not one word and staring at the white wall in front of me.

"He's in shock right now," Nate said. "But his mother has been missing for almost four months."

"Why didn't anyone report it?"

Nate really couldn't explain, and I wasn't willing to. "He . . . he just thought she'd come back, and didn't know if she was out of town with relatives."

"Who else lives here? Why didn't anyone notice the smell? Do you know of anyone who would have wanted her dead?"

Poetry inched forward, but I grabbed her wrist and gave her a cold stare. I'd told her a lot of things, but I did not want her talking to the police about what had gone down. She sat back, shaking her head.

"Do you have something to say?" one of the officers asked her.

"No, nothing at all. This is just . . . just awful," she said, starting to cry again.

The officer looked at me. "Jamal, if you don't talk, we can't help you. I know you're upset right now, but if you can think of anything that will help us find the person who murdered your mother we would appreciate it. I don't know why you're not talking to us but you, yourself, don't want to be our suspect. If you know something, you need to come clean and do it soon."

I ignored the officer, and cocked my neck from side to side.

"He'll be willin' to talk later," Nate said. "Just give him time."

The officer put his foot on the table and tapped his notepad. "I got a dead woman in a trash bag and nobody knows nothing? Give me a break, people. All we're here to do is help. Now, if you don't mind, we're going to finish our investigation, look around, and see what we can find. Don't any of you go nowhere until we're finished."

He and the other officers walked away, searching through the house as well as outside to see what they could find. Nate sat next to me on the couch.

"You got to be smart about this, Prince. Go ahead and tell them what you suspect about Raylo. That way, it will take the heat off you. You know they're goin' to come after you as a prime suspect, especially if they don't find any evidence. Listen to what I'm tellin' you, man, and get that revenge shit out of yo' head right now because it's not gon' work this time."

*Like hell,* was all I could say to myself. Raylo was a dead fool and didn't even know. And if I found G, he was a goner too. Somebody had to pay for this, and how in the hell did he think he could get away with killing Mama? He must have mistaken me for being a punk-ass fool, but I had something major planned for that ass. I got hyped just sitting there and thinking about it.

As the police continued to tear up the house looking for evidence, I heard a bunch of yelling going on outside. It moved me not one bit, because I knew whose voice it was. It was Raylo. He rushed inside with one of his friends holding him back. Tears poured from his eyes and beads of sweat laced his forehead.

"What in the hell happened to my Shante?" he said to one of the officers who tried to calm him down. The officer asked for his name.

"My name don't matter," he yelled. "Where in the hell is my baby? Who did this to her, damn it, who?"

My eyes focused on him, with daggers tearing him apart. He finally turned to see me sitting on the couch, and had the audacity to come over by me.

"Prince," he said with his face all frowned up and looking like a fake-ass mad bulldog. He was bent over, holding his back as if it was hurting. "Who the fuck did this? Why they do this to her, man? You know this shit ain't right!"

I sat there eyeing him, showing no emotions whatsoever. Poetry was just as still as I was, not knowing what I was going to do.

Nate jumped up and grabbed Raylo's hand. "I know this is hard on you both, but let's calm down and see if we can figure this out later. The police are here, and for now, let's allow them to do their job."

Raylo's whole demeanor changed, as he was now standing up straight. "Nigga, who the fuck are you? Do I know you?"

"I'm a friend of Prince's. Work at the liquor store for him. My name is Nate."

"Aw," Raylo said, squeezing his forehead. He pulled a handkerchief from his pocket and blew his pug nose.

I know he saw me staring at him, and as my brows arched inward, he blinked to look away. He tapped one of the police officer's shoulders and started talking to him, as if he was so concerned.

"What y'all gon' do about this? I want Shante's killer found and y'all need to get on it!"

His performance was so damn good, but I could see right through it. Just like he acted at Ernie's house, he was acting the same way. The officer started asking Raylo questions, and he gave more details about Mama's disappearance than I had.

"She just up and left one day. We had an argument the day before, and she told me she was gettin' the hell out of here. Shante was known for runnin' off like that for long periods of time, but none of us suspected that she was here all along. Dead."

He knew she was here all along, and in G's own words, he also said she's at home where she had been all along. G had also referred to Raylo as Ray. At the time I didn't trip, but only close friends of his called him Ray.

Raylo got choked up again. I wanted to just get up and beat his fake ass! Poetry saw the devious look in my eyes and she reached for my hand to hold it.

"I know you told me to shut the fuck up, but can I get you anything to drink? It's been a long day, Prince, and I'm so sorry about all of this. I'm right here with you, though, so don't worry, baby. We'll get through this together, okay?"

No response. She was saying that shit now, but I wondered if she would be singing the same tune after all of this was done and over with. Yeah, I couldn't wait, and as I sucked my teeth, my gaze stayed right on Raylo. I wanted him to see that killer look in my eyes. He needed to see how hungry I was for him. I wanted him to fidget as he was doing, and his shifty eyes were trying to ignore me. He couldn't, as I wouldn't let him. And when one of the police officers came into the house with what he called "evidence" in a bag, Raylo really showed out.

"You think you got somethin'?" he said in a panic to the officer.

Raylo looked guilty as ever, but I wasn't sure if the police noticed it as much as I had. Nate poked me in my side, as he noticed the bullshit too.

"We're not sure," the officer said. "But we're done here." He walked over to me and reached out his hand for me to shake it. "Sorry for your loss. We'll be in touch."

I looked at his hand, refusing to shake it. Nate shoved my side again, then reached out for the officer's hand. "Thank you, sir. We appreciate your efforts."

"I hope so," the officer said, then left out with the others.

Raylo and his friend watched the officers leave, then he came over to me. "We need to get with the funeral home and make sure Shante is appropriately laid to rest. I don't recall her ever talkin' about havin' a life insurance policy or anything like that, but you may know somethin' better than I do. If push comes to shove, I'll take care of everything. You don't have to worry about nothin', ya hear me?"

I stood up, stepped over the table to avoid him, and walked away. I heard Nate say, "Give him time." After that, I went into my bedroom and closed the door. I could still smell Mama's smoky scent all over, and trying to cope with the fact that she was gone, I couldn't. I placed my hand on my chest, sobbing like I had never done in my entire life, while lying on my bed. The loss of Mama, and the way she went out, indeed, was painful.

# Chapter Thirteen

## Missing Mama

All I had arranged for Mama was a viewing of her casket then she would be laid to rest at the cemetery. It's what she wanted, and the life insurance policy she had paid for her funeral, and left me with $20,000. Her house now belonged to me, but eventually, I was going to sell it. There were good memories there, but I really felt as if the bad outweighed the good. All I thought about was growing up in that room. Listening to Mama get her ass beat, and crying and arguing with the numerous men in her life. Her situation with Raylo took the cake though. I never understood how a woman could take so much heat from a man, but still love him. Her love for him eventually cost her her life, and whatever happened that night between her and Raylo, no one would ever know.

Still, I had to hang on to the good times with Mama: the times she used to read me bedtime stories and take me to church, sit on my bed with me and talk until the sun came up, even drink and smoke weed with me. Yes, we did have our fun. When Prince Jr. was born, Mama was like a new woman. She was excited about seeing him, and more so about seeing me. Our relationship had gotten back on track but, now, another person in my life had been snatched away from me. Yes, I knew there was a God. But, I didn't always understand how

He went about doing things. I guess I prayed for Him to reveal to me where Mama was, and just like in my dream, it was revealed the next day that she was dead. I was thankful for Him allowing her to finally rest in peace, and as I sat in a pew in the funeral home, looking at her pearly white casket, I wasn't satisfied with the hand that life had dealt me. At times, it had been too much to bear, but I knew that a Street Soldier like me had to keep it moving.

As I sat in my black pants, shirt, and tie from Express Men, I watched as more people came in to pay Mama their respects. I opted to keep her casket closed, only because there was nothing but ashes inside. Her body was badly decomposed, so she was cremated. A beautiful picture of her sat on top of the casket. The people who came by were from the neighborhood, and some from the nightclubs she'd frequent when she went out. Mama had no siblings and the only family we pretty much had was each other. Some of my friends from high school stopped by, and so did some of my customers from the liquor store and laundromat. Jenay and Francine both came by, which kind of surprised me. I kept my conversation short, but shook a lot of hands, thanking many for coming. When I looked up and saw Poetry and her grandmother coming my way, I let out a tiny smile. I stood up, offering her grandmother a seat, since the room was pretty full.

"No, you go ahead and sit down," she whispered while holding on to a cane.

"No, I insist. Besides, I need to go to the bathroom."

She kissed my cheek, then eased herself into the seat. Poetry squeezed my hand together with hers, and she was really a sight for sore eyes to see. She wore a pink chiffon sheer dress that had spaghetti straps. The dress was cut right above her knees and her perfume was just

as sweet as her. A pink and white flower was in her hair
and the same flower was on her finger, as she wore it as
a ring. The open-toed strappy heels she wore had her
almost as tall as me.

"How are you feeling?" she asked, walking with me
to the restroom, with her head leaning against my
shoulder.

"I'm okay," I said. "Thanks for bein' here. That was
sweet of you to bring your grandmother."

"Hey, we're like two peas in a pod. Wherever I go,
she goes."

"She wasn't in the bedroom with us the other night.
That was you making all of those noises."

Poetry blushed and pushed my shoulder. "Shhh,
don't tell nobody. And there are certain places I prefer
to be alone. With you is one of them and I refuse to
share."

I smiled. Hadn't done so all day, but I knew Poetry
could take me there. I loosened my hand from hers and
made my way into the bathroom. I didn't really have
to go, I just needed a minute to gather myself, as well
as my thoughts. I looked in the mirror, seeing so much
stress on my face. Small bags were underneath my eyes
and in no way did I look my age. I'd be twenty-one in a
few more weeks, and it was a shame that all of this had
to happen right before my birthday.

Trying to cool off, I splashed cold water on my face,
then dabbed it with a paper towel. I left the bathroom
and walked back to the room where Mama was. As
soon as I stepped inside, I spotted Raylo and about ten
of his friends. Some were sitting down, others were
standing close by Mama's casket. One of them was
saying something, and Raylo took it upon himself to
laugh. He barely looked my way, and as I kept staring
at him, Poetry turned my face to hers.

"Now ain't the time," she said to me. "Let it go, Prince, and stop staring at him. Too many people are watching. I don't want you and him to start tripping at a time like this. This day is all about your mother. Make her proud, okay?"

I chilled, for now, but it wouldn't be for too long. Poetry, her grandmother, and I rode together in a limo to the cemetery, and as we followed Mama's hearse, my emotions got the best of me. I tried to hold them in all day, but couldn't contain myself no more. I leaned over in the seat, holding my stomach from the ill feeling I felt inside. Poetry's grandmother rubbed my leg, then pulled me up to hold me in her arms.

"Aww, baby, it's gon' be okay. We all have to get out of here someday, and your mother is in a much, much better place. She's saying hallelujah right now and she's so happy that she's now in God's care. Nobody's care is better than His, so wipe those tears and be thankful that your mother is free as she would ever want to be."

"That's right, Prince," Poetry said, moving next to me. She squeezed my hand again. "I love you. And I know you're going to keep doing your mother proud. We gon' do it together and think about everything that the future holds."

I guessed I wasn't seeing it like they were right now. I was full of anger and bitterness. Needless to say, my future wasn't looking good. Satisfaction for me would only come when Raylo was being driven to the cemetery in his hearse and I knew that day was coming soon.

Everyone stood around the gravesite, listening to the funeral director speak. One of Raylo's friends was talking loud, and everyone knew he was drunk. Raylo looked pretty high, too, and he stared at Mama's casket with tears running down his face. He looked over at me, and you best believe that my eyes were on him. Even when everyone bowed their heads to pray, our eyes stayed connected. His eye twitched, and he winked it. That, in itself, pissed me the fucked off, but I remained calm.

"This now concludes our services," the funeral director said. "And if anyone would like any flowers, please feel free to take some."

Everyone started reaching for flowers, including me. Raylo gathered in a circle with his friends, and they were talking, as well as laughing. Poetry's grandmother headed back to the limo, and I stood around, shaking hands and saying good-bye to those who came.

"Take care of yourself, Prince," one lady said who I didn't know.

One of Mama's longtime friends, Barbara, gave me a hug and wiped her eyes. She squeezed my cheek. "Boy, I am going to miss your crazy-ass mama. I really hate this happened, Prince, but you gon' be all right. That's all yo' mama ever talked about was you, and she loved her little Prince. I hope you know that."

"I do," I said, getting choked up again. Sometimes, people didn't know when to cut it off. All of this was really too much.

The crowd became scarce, and Poetry and I started to walk back to the limo. When I turned around, though, I saw Raylo and two of his friends standing close by Mama's casket and watching it lower to the ground. I stood for a moment to watch, and even though Poetry thought I was watching the casket go down, I was really watching Raylo. I wanted to get his attention, and right after he blew Mama a kiss, he looked up at me. I positioned my finger like a gun and aimed it at him. He snickered and I read his lips as he spoke to his friend.

"That dumb motherfucka crazy," he clearly said.

With that, I headed toward him, but Poetry grabbed my arm. I snatched away from her, charging in Raylo's direction. Poetry stood in front of me, trying to push me back with all the strength she had.

"No, Prince, no! Stop this, please! Let him be! Don't do this!"

I was so mad that I pushed her hard, knocking her on her ass. She rushed up and pulled me by my shirt, tearing it.

"Will you listen to me?" she screamed.

"Move yo' ass out of the way," I yelled back.

The people around us were looking, trying to see what was going on, because I had pushed her away from me again. This time, she fell in some mud and it splashed on her pink dress. I kept it moving toward Raylo with nothing but rage in my eyes. When I reached him, he thought I had words for him, but that wasn't the case. He held out his hands, and as he opened his mouth, I pushed his ass so hard that he slipped and fell backward into the six-foot hole with Mama.

"Oh my God!" Mama's friend Barbara shouted. "Stop that, Prince! This is awful!"

"Somebody get him," another person said from afar.

"Priiiiiince," I could hear Poetry yell.

Several people started running toward me, and two of Raylo's friends held me back. We tussled until I broke loose. I pointed my finger down at Raylo as he tried to climb out, but couldn't get a grip on the slippery mud. "Nigga, that's where you'll be real soon," I threatened. "Get comfortable and I'll be seein' you in a minute."

One of Raylo's partners shoved me away and reached down to help Raylo. It definitely was no easy task, and by the time he was out, I was being held back by three men from the funeral home.

"Come on, man. Why you disrespecting your mama like that? Get in this damn car and let's go."

The older man chimed in too, wiping the sweat from his head with a handkerchief. "I tell you! These young kids are out of control these days. What is the world coming to?"

I was put into the limo, and the chauffer quickly pulled off. I watched Raylo covered in mud and cursing his ass off. Poetry sat across from me, being held and consoled by her grandmother, who was rubbing her arm and telling her it would be okay. She looked mad as hell, and her cold stare was intimidating. Poetry sniffled and not once did she look my way. I felt like shit, but I told her to move out of my way. She should have known better than to interfere, but even so, nothing justified what I had done.

I looked over at her and her grandmother. "I'm sorry," was all I could say.

"Sorry?" her grandmother said through clinched teeth. "If you ever treat her like that again, I will break your neck with my bare hands."

I had no comeback for her words, and as for Poetry, she had no words either.

When we got back to the funeral home, the limo dropped us off at our cars. Poetry walked with her grandmother to her car, and I walked slowly beside them. "Did you hear me?" I asked her. "I said I was sorry. I didn't mean for that to happen, but I couldn't help myself." Seeing her cry truly broke my heart.

"Whatever, Prince. Whatever."

She helped her grandmother get into the car, and I stood with my hands in my pockets as they drove away. God, I felt so bad, but maybe this was for the best.

# Chapter Fourteen

### Don't Take It Personal . . .
### Then Again, Please Do

I hadn't heard from Poetry in a week, so I figured our relationship was a wrap. I'd been keeping up with my plans, and that was to find a way to catch Raylo slipping. That, I did. For the past two nights, I'd been following his every move. He'd bought himself a new Cadillac, I assumed with the money I had given to G. I'd seen him, too. He and Raylo had met up at a house on the south side with two white females. One was the woman I'd known as Peaches, and the other I had never seen before. I guessed she was Mama's replacement.

Either way, they'd had a routine going on. One that I had been following very well, and when I drove by earlier, I saw Raylo drop one of the women off. I knew he'd be coming back for her later, and if G was with him, I would kill two birds with one stone. Four, if the ladies didn't wish to cooperate.

Deciding to tie up my loose ends, around 7:00 P.M. I went over to the liquor store to holla at Nate. I had to make somebody aware of what was going down, just in case things didn't go according to my plan.

"I really wish you wouldn't go through with this, Prince, and if there is anything that I can say or do to stop you, tell me what it is. The fact that the police was able to find the knife that killed your mama says to me that an arrest may be comin' soon. Why don't you wait to see how all of this will play out before you do anything?"

"I don't have faith in the police to do anything, and since I suspect they are on G's payroll like many drug dealers are, I doubt that anything will be done. Besides, I need to get this off my chest and it's the only way I know how to. I'm gon' lay low for a while. I need you to keep the laundromat and liquor store goin' for me, because I'll need the money. I'll give you whatever you want, just be sure to take care of this for me."

"You know I will," he said, taking a moment to pause and feeling the need to lecture me. "A long time ago, I was young and had an attitude like you too. Couldn't nobody tell me nothin', so I'm done tryin' to stop you from doin' what you gon' do. Just be careful and call me when you make it to your destination."

"I will," I said, slamming my hand against his. "In a minute."

Nate pulled me in for a tight hug, then patted my back. "You're really goin' to go through with this, aren't you?"

"Yes. I have to do this for Mama."

Nate rubbed his chin, shaking his head. "I can't let you do this, Prince. I wish you would have told me a long time ago that G's real name is Geronimo. He and I go way back. Did some time together in prison, but had a small beef while we were in there. We still speak to each other, though, and even though I can't believe I'm saying this to you right now, especially after all of that bullshit I just said, I can't let you go through this alone. Let me make a few phone calls, and if you want your man, I'll bring him to you."

"Nate, don't play. I hope this ain't some kind of joke you're playin', just so I don't go through with this. The only way it's not goin' to happen is if you kill me right now. I'm not sure if you want to do that, so just let me be."

Nate paced the floor and sighed. "This is no joke." He looked at his watch. "Give me about an hour. Go home, take a load off, and wait until I call you. When I do, I'll be talkin' in riddles and shit, but that'll be my cue for you to come back over. Use your key to get in and you'll be able to say whatever you want to to G. After that, we'll go from there."

"I . . . I really don't want to put you in the middle of this, Nate. I know you're tryin' to keep your life on the right path and that's why I didn't want to tell you about what was goin' on, because I didn't want to involve you in my mess. Every time I involve somebody they get hurt. Trust me, I got this."

Nate grabbed my shoulder and squeezed it. "I know you got it, and I got your back too. So, go over to your apartment like I told you to and wait for my call."

A tiny part of me was skeptical, only because G had set me up and so had Raylo. I trusted Nate with everything that I owned, but at the end of the day, black men were known for snaking real bad. I had to keep that in the back of my mind, and as I crossed over the street to go into my apartment, I tried not to think about Nate being on that level. I had been crossed too many times before, and when my boy Cedric had set me the hell up that day, it lead to something I never thought I'd have to deal with. I stood with my hands in my pockets, leaning against the building and thinking about the day I would always remember as the biggest betrayal of my life.

*Cedric and I had just left a pizza joint that day, where we had entertained some girls from high school and had played some video games. I was walking with him to the car I had purchased for him, truly feeling as if he was the only friend I had in Romeo's absence. We slammed hands together, and as he got on his way, I opened the door to my car, only to be approached by a brotha dark as midnight, asking if I had a light.*

*"Nah, bruh," I said, gazing into his sneaky eyes. I knew what a thief in the night looked like, but before I could open my car door, he made a move. He pulled out a shiny blade, holding it to my throat. My arm was being twisted behind my back and the way he held it caused severe pain to shoot up my arm.*

*"Up your wallet and empty yo' pockets, nigga! If you make a false move, I'll cut yo' gotdamn throat!"*

*The blade was pinching my neck, so I was careful not to trip. I reached in my pocket, then dropped my wallet on the ground. He dug in my pockets, and put the wad of money I had into his pocket. He then punched me in my stomach, tearing up my gut with powerful blows. I fell to the ground, and all I could feel were the soldier marks he was delivering to my body. I could barely move, and my body was starting to feel numb. I shielded my face with my hands, but as he kept stomping me, my face and hands bounced against the concrete. Lying there helpless, I saw the nigga open my car door and check my car.*

*The first place he looked was underneath my seat. Moments later, he came out with the bag of money I'd kept underneath there. He opened the glove compartment, and inside of there he found my platinum chain. I was so afraid that he'd see my silencer underneath the passenger's seat, but his head jerked up when he heard a man ask if I needed some help.*

*"Yessss," I strained with blood gushing from my mouth. The brotha jumped out of the car, and just for the hell of it, he kicked his foot that was laced up with*

*green and white Air Jordans right in my face. It felt
like my neck had been separated from my body, and
all I heard were his footsteps running away. I rolled
on my back, staring up at the dark sky. I had no idea
how badly I was hurt, but the man rushed over to help
me.*

*"I'm going inside to call 911. Hang in there, brotha,"
he said.*

*In no way did I want the police on the scene. I had
my silencer in the car, and finding that alone would
send me to jail. I eased up, tightly gripping my midsection. Slowly making my way to my feet, I sat in my
car, trying to get myself together. I could feel what
my face looked like, and I used my shirt to wipe down
it. A whole lot of blood covered my shirt and my face
burned like hell; not as much as my stomach was
burning but, unfortunately, I wasn't up to visiting no
doctor.*

*I had a gut feeling about this shit, a feeling that led
me to Cedric's house. I parked down his street, waiting to see if he showed. His car wasn't there yet, but
I knew it would soon come. I slid down in my seat,
resting my head against the window. I was hurting
so bad, and I hoped like hell that my suspicions didn't
pan out to be true.*

*Almost an hour later, Cedric pulled in front of his
house. He went inside, but nearly twenty minutes after that, another car pulled up. There were two niggas
inside, and after the driver blew the horn, Cedric came
outside. The first thing I saw when the driver stepped
out of the car was his green and white Air Jordans.
Something horrible went through me, and this was
why I didn't like hanging with a bunch of fake-ass niggas. Cedric had set my ass up good, or so he thought.
He was gon' pay for this shit. He and his friends sat*

*outside for a minute, smoking a blunt and laughing. I actually saw dude describing how he stomped my ass on the ground and he laughed hard as he must have been describing his final blow to my face. He slapped hands with Cedric, and with the joint dangling from the ol' boy's mouth, I saw him count out some money, putting it into Cedric's hand. Afterward, Cedric put up his fist and hurried inside. The other two fellas got in the car and drove off.*

*Knowing exactly how much was stolen from me, I was down to less than a hundred Gs. They took the bulk of my money, as I really hadn't been spending much at all. I should have known better than to keep my money underneath the seat. I thought it was tucked away pretty good. The rest was at home in my closet, but I really didn't feel safe with it being there. The landlord had a key to get inside whenever he wanted to, and there really was no other place that I could keep it. Mama's house was not an option, and as much as she snooped around, I was sure she would find it. For now, I intended to leave the rest of my money exactly where it was, and never again would I keep that much money on me.*

*Fifteen minutes had gone by, and that was when I called Cedric.*

*"Say, man," I said in a soft tone.*

*"Who dis?"*

*"Prince. It's Prince."*

*"What's up, bro?"*

*"After you left the pizza joint, I got robbed. Ol' boy fucked me up, Ced, and I'm at my mama's house right now. She gon' take me to the hospital, but I need you to do somethin' for me."*

*"I will, but are you okay? I mean, how bad are your injuries? You talkin' about goin' to the hospital and you soundin' like you on your last breath."*

*"I feel like it too, but, uh, that nigga got me for al-most two hundred grand," I lied. "I saw him dump some of it in the dumpster behind the pizza joint. Maybe he was hidin' it from somebody, but see if it's still there for me. I can't even move right now, and I feel like my ribs are cracked."*

*"Damn, Prince, that shit fucked up. I'll go check it out for you, and if it's there, you know I got you. We gon' find out who that nigga was, so don't worry about it right now. Be well and I'll get at you later about the money."*

*"Thanks, bruh. Thanks."*

*I hung up, knowing that Cedric would be leaving, thinking he'd got swindled by his friends. Sure enough, he left his house, flying to get to the dumpster behind the pizza joint. I followed several car lengths behind him, and watched as he parked beside the dumpster. His head was down, and as he was searching through the dumpster, I started his way in my car. My bright lights were beaming, and I could see him squinting. He put his hand over his eyes to shield the brightness. But, by then, my silencer was already out of the win-dow. I fired off one shot that instantly dropped him. Just to be sure that he was hit, I slowly got out of the car, pumping more shots into his chest and busting it wide open.*

After that day, I felt as if no one could be trusted. I didn't want, nor did I need, any so-called friends. All I could think was Nate better not cross me, and God help him if he did.

I went upstairs to my apartment, closed the door, and tossed my keys on the table. I started to lift some weights to occupy the time, but I could only do so much lifting. I wanted so badly to call Poetry, but I was in no mood to listen to her tell me what I should or should

not be doing. I missed her already and I hated that I
had brought her into something that I wasn't ready for.
Even so, the phone was still in my hand. I punched a
few numbers, only to hit the end button shortly thereafter.

I stood, pacing the floor and cracking my knuckles.
I wondered how Nate was going to get G in my sights,
and what I would do when I was finally face-to-face
with him. Did the money even matter to me anymore? I
regretted not telling Nate about G sooner, as this could
have been done and over with a long time ago. But now
it seemed as if the opportunity was about to present
itself, and I was ready. I rubbed my hands together,
and finally took a seat on the couch. My cell phone was
on the table, and all I did was stare at it, waiting for it
to ring.

Almost like clockwork, a little over an hour later, my
cell phone rang. It was Nate.

"Ay, man. I got G here with your package. He wants
ten grand for it, and unless you got it, don't waste his
time. Meet me at my apartment and he'll be here until
you get here. And you already know the rules. Don't
bring nobody with you."

"On my way."

I popped up from my seat, checking my Glock again,
making sure there were enough bullets inside. There
were, so I tucked the gun down inside of my pants. I
made my way across the street to Nate's apartment,
already seeing the sign on the liquor store that said it
was closed. I used my key to open his door in the back,
then slowly walked up the red painted wooden stairs
that took me to the upper level. The old steps creaked
and I had my hand on my gun, careful, just in case
this was another setup. I could hear G and Nate talking, laughing a few times, and then someone coughed.

When I reached the top of the stairs, I saw the back of G standing against the kitchen counter. A leather brown jacket was tightened around all that fat and his beard was even more rugged. Thick fat bulged on the back of his neck and his bald head had plenty of dents. I could have taken him out right then and there, but I wanted him to see me. I wanted him to tell me that, for a fact, Raylo was my man. There was little doubt, but I just wanted to be sure.

Nate and G were sipping on something that had been poured into Styrofoam cups. When I crept up from behind, Nate's sneaky eyes looked over G's shoulder. By then, I was already next to him with my Glock pointing at his head.

"Long time no see," I said. "Now, tell me. What the fuck happen to my mama and to my money? And if you got any of my dough on you, I'll take it."

G smirked, then looked at Nate. "Man, I didn't think you had this kind of shit in you. Did you really try to play me like this? After all I did for you while in prison, nigga, this is how you repay me? And for this chump?"

Nate said not one word, but I spoke up. "I got your chump. He's comin' real soon. Now answer my questions, fool."

"G, somethin' tells me that you'd better answer the almighty Prince," Nate said. "I've never considered him as no chump, and I think you may have underestimated my li'l nigga. As for prison, that was a long time ago. I saved yo' ass plenty of times too, but I'm not sure if I will be able to save you today."

"You's a dirty motherfucka," G said to Nate. "And if you think you will not pay for this shit, you're sadly mistaken. Do you know how many niggas know that I'm over here? If I don't show up tonight, they gon' come lookin' for me. I can't believe you've injected

yourself in this shit, my friend, and your decision to do
so will be costly."

Nate chuckled, then looked at me. "He's talkin' too
much shit. If you're not goin' to handle yo' business
with him, I will. Hurry up, 'cause I got a job that I need
to get back to."

I was straight up feeling Nate, and shame on me for
feeling as if he didn't have my back. This nigga had it
and then some. I hadn't ever met nobody like him before, and it felt good to have him on my team. I turned
my gun to the side.

"Hold up!" G said, moving a few inches away from
me. His forehead was filled with hot beads of sweat
already. "I'm not yo' man, young blood. You need to
know right now that I was not the nigga who killed yo'
mama. If you let me walk out that door alive, I'll tell
you what the fuck happened, fasho."

"Go," I said. "You got one minute to speak, then I'll
decide if I'm gon' let you walk."

"I need to know for sure. I'll take you to the nigga
who did it, but I need your word that you won't kill
me."

"Got it. And as long as you take me to the nigga who
did it, I'm good," I said. "Now speak."

He hesitated for a few seconds, then his snitching
ass spoke up. "I got a call from yo' stepfather, tellin' me
that—"

I got antsy, and pushed the tip of the gun against his
temple. "That nigga ain't my step daddy. Clear that shit
up!"

"I mean Raylo. Raylo . . . he knew where we could
get some extra cash. Said that he'd give me twenty-five
grand if I played along with his plan. At first, I didn't
know what he'd done to yo' mama, until he told me that
they'd got into an argument and she got jiggy with him.

He slapped her so hard with his gun that she fell backward and hit her head on the edge of the kitchen table. He thought she was unconscious, and he left her on the floor to chill out. Then, when the nigga came back, he realized she wasn't breathin'. He panicked and didn't want to go to jail. He had to dispose of her body, and from what that fool told me, he cut up her body, and put it in a plastic bag. He never told me exactly where it was, but insisted that it was somewhere in the house. So, this was an accident. . . ."

Tears welled in my eyes as I listened to G. "Accident? Nigga, you don't cut up nobody's damn body by accident! What the fuck are you talkin' about?"

G was trembling all over, trying to calm me, but couldn't even calm himself. "I mean the initial blow was an accident. Now, that nigga was wrong for what he did to her body. I told him that, too, and he should have just said somethin' to you . . . somebody about what happened. Now we're all in too deep and I never thought it would come down to me possibly losing my life by the hands of a Street Soldier. We don't need to go out like this, do we?"

"Maybe so. But you need to keep tellin' me what's up. Where the fuck is my money?"

G moved his head from side to side. "Prince, I know what I'm sayin' to you doesn't minimize yo' pain, but shit happens."

I pushed his temple again with the gun and he squeezed his eyes together. "You're right. Shit will happen if you don't get to the point and tell me what the hell happened to my money!"

He sighed. "The money . . . You'd have to get most of that back from him. I can't tell you what I spent my dollars on, but we can make some arrangements for you to get some of it back. I will make sure that you do, and if you allow me a little more time, I may be able to get you more than what you put up. So, think about it. Do we have a deal or what?"

"I don't make deals with snake-ass niggas like you, G. And while you may have told me some of the truth here today, I just don't believe that you will follow through with what you're saying. Somethin' about your words don't ring true to me and I think that, given the opportunity, you would get out of dodge and make sure Raylo is in a safe place, too. No way in hell I'ma let that happen."

G moved his head from side to side and stamped his foot hard on the ground, trying to make his case. "You have my word! And anyone who knows me, they know my word is bond! Let's stop wastin' time and go get the nigga who is responsible for this. It's time to put this shit to rest and I know you will feel so much better. Once I put yo' money back into your hand, we can wash this situation down the drain."

I stood, looking back and forth at Nate and G. Nate was biting into a crunchy apple, waiting for me to respond. I was speechless, torn, on the ropes about what to do. The gun was shaking in my hand, but the anxiousness that I felt to shoot him wasn't there. I cocked my neck from side to side, trying to get out of him all that I could. "Who . . . who the fuck is Monroe? How in the hell did he fit into all of this shit?"

"Monroe? I . . . I don't know nobody named Monroe."

"The fool who lives in Kansas City. I found his name, number, and addy on my mama's dresser. Who put it there?"

"Ray did. He knew you'd be snooping around and he wanted to throw you off. The brotha in Kansas City, his name wasn't Monroe. It was Carter. Raylo paid him to tell you that your mama had been there, but he had

never met yo' mama. See, that nigga had to cover his
tracks. He got all of us involved in his shit and we're the
ones who have to answer for this, not him. I say let's
all go get that motherfucka and make him pay. If you
kill me, you'll be killin' the wrong man. I just did what
I was asked to do for a little bit of change that wasn't
much to brag on. So think about it, Prince. Is it gon' be
me, or him? All I ask is that you not do somethin' you'll
regret."

I was speechless, again, and slowly lowered my gun.
I was so damn upset with Raylo that I had lost focus on
dealing with G. I wanted to run out of there and go blow
that nigga's brains out, and I knew that killing G would
definitely bring more heat my way. How much heat
was the question? Did I want to continue living my life
on the run, running from niggas who had fucked me
over or made bad decisions to help out someone else?
I wasn't so sure. I was skeptical, and at least this fool
had told me the truth. Or, had he? There were always
two . . . three sides to every story, and no matter how I
looked at it, this fool had poked his nose where it didn't
belong. Nate interrupted my thoughts.

"Wait a minute," he said, walking closer to us and
taking another bite of his apple. "You mean to tell me
that all of this was an accident? Raylo didn't try to kill
Shante?"

G nodded. "That's exactly what I'm sayin'. You and
I both know that accidents happen all the time, but he
shouldn't have asked me to get involved in this. I can't
take that shit back, but again, I can hand the man you
really and truly want over to you on a silver platter."

After that, Nate moved so quick that I barely had
time to think. He snatched the gun from my hand, and
before I knew it, he had the tip of the gun against G's
temple. Without a blink, Nate pulled the trigger, splat-
tering G's brains right there in the kitchen.

"Accidents do happen," Nate said, watching G's heavy body drop to the floor. Nate looked at me, standing there, stunned. "Too much talkin' and not enough action. Get out of here and let me clean up this mess. You already know the play. You ain't seen nothin', you don't know nothin', and you ain't heard nothin'."

I was frozen . . . still in shock about what Nate had done. I wanted to ask him what was up, but decided to do as I was told. Of course, that was a first. As I made my way to the door, Nate called my name. I turned around.

"What's up?" I asked.

"He was the nigga who I went to jail for. This shit was personal and it was a long time comin'. As for Raylo, you go do what you have to do."

He reached out to give me my Glock back, and I eased it from his hand. "At least you kept your word to him and didn't shoot him, huh?"

"Yea . . . yeah," I stuttered. "But my word ain't shit."

"Mine either," he laughed.

I left, thinking about all these so-called people known as friends. You could sholl find yourself fucked up, and it was evident that beefs among niggas could last a long, long time.

Feeling unsafe, I didn't want to go back to my apartment right now. Instead, I drove to the hotel where I had planned to stay the night, just in case somebody came looking for me. Of course, I didn't want to be found, especially since I now knew for a fact that Raylo was my man, and I suspected where he was. After I handled my business with him, I planned to chill for a couple of days to let the dust settle.

While in the hotel room, I glided my fingers against my Glock, then aimed it at the mirror. I pretended to shoot, then laid the gun on the bed. I closed my eyes, thinking about what Raylo had done to Mama. If what G said was true, I couldn't believe he'd cut up her body like that. What kind of animal was he? How could he do that shit to a woman he claimed to love? Was this the kind of man Mama allowed to be in our lives all this time? This shit was mad crazy, and some damn women just didn't know what kind of shit they were getting themselves into.

I watched the clock tick away, then popped up. This had been one crazy-ass day, but it was now time for me to handle mine, like Nate had handled his. I hoped like hell that no one would get after him, but Nate was good at covering his tracks. He had me fooled, thinking that he'd turned over a new leaf. I felt him, though, and when business had to be handled, it just had to be handled.

My gun was in my possession and I flipped my black hoodie over my head. It was cold as hell outside, so I eased my hands into a pair of black leather gloves, rubbing my hands together. I got in my car, thinking about Mama, my future, and about the only chick that I could honestly say I ever really loved, Miss Poetry. My mind flashed back to the first day I'd met her and how brave and sassy she was. I thought about her truly trying to be there for me, and she was one person who definitely had my back. Sex with her was the best and no chick had ever taken me to the level she did. I couldn't get the thought of me pushing her to the ground out of my head. How dare I just offer her a simple "sorry"? After tonight, I didn't know what was going to happen. G, as well as Raylo, had some connections that would surely make me, and possibly Nate, pay for what had gone down and what was about to. I could face either death or possibly jail time after this. It didn't look good for me at all, but I had to stop to see my Poetry, just in case I would never see her again.

I parked in front of her grandmother's house, seeing Poetry sitting on the porch. It was dark outside, but I knew it was her. She was on the swing with some papers and a pen in her hand. I walked up the steps and she folded the papers, putting them next to her.

"What you writin'?" I asked, sitting next to her on the swing.

"I was writing you a letter," she said. "I hadn't gotten far with it, but I was preparing myself to send it to you in prison."

I looked down and clinched my hands together. "Don't burn no bread on me like that. You don't know what's goin' to happen to me."

"I don't, but I'm preparing myself for the worst because your mind is so far gone that you won't listen to anyone right now. I wish you would just listen!"

"I'm sorry that you don't understand what all of this is about, but I didn't come over here for you to talk me out of what I'm about to do. I just wanted to tell you that I was sorry, again, for hurtin' you, and that I appreciate everything that you've done for me. I ain't ever had nobody in my life like you, Poetry, and all of this was really new to me. But I told you from the beginnin' that I had some deep shit goin' on. Relationships had no place in my life. I hope you see, now, why I felt that way."

"But why keep living that way, Prince? Why must you keep doin' the same things over and over? At some point, you have to be willing to make some changes. You say you want a better life, but you keep traveling down the same ol' path. All I wanted you to see was that you had a different path to choose. I asked you to take that route with me, but you don't want it. I'm not going to keep worrying myself about this, and if your mind is made up, then you go ahead and do what you gotta do. I love you and I wish you all the best."

I stood up, not wanting to waste much more time. "Some people and their situations never change, Poetry. I think that may very well apply to me. Thanks for holdin' me down and keepin' me grounded while you could."

I bent over to kiss her, surprised that she kissed me back. It wasn't for long, though, then she backed away. "Do you want your letter?" she asked, holding out the papers to me.

"Nah, save it. Send it to me when I reach my destination, whatever that destination may be."

I jogged down the steps, and being the fighter that she was, she ran after me. "I can't send it to you if you're six feet under. Just think about what I'm saying to you, please. I know that you need more than somebody to love you right now but, Prince, it's all I got. I need you, too, and I don't want anything to happen to you. Losing you will break my heart into pieces and you've got to hear me out. Let this go for me. Let it go for us. I really think we can do this and I'm going to help you all I can. I can't help you, though, if you want to continue to run around here like a madman. It ain't the way, baby, it truly ain't the way."

What Poetry was saying, and had been saying all along, was going in one ear and out the other. I wished she could have understood the kind of person I was. It would make it so much easier for her. "I don't have much time to respond to all of that you just said. But I can't do this for you, Poetry, I have to do this for me. Nobody killed yo' mama like they did mine. You haven't been hurt like me and fucked around time and time again. Yeah, you've been through some shit, but nothin' like what I've been through. That's why you don't get it. You'll never get it and the only reason I came here tonight was to make peace with you. I'm sorry I let you in, but it was a big mistake for me to do that. I had a feelin' it would resort to me fallin' in love wit' you and losin' you all at the same time. But that's how the story of my life goes."

I walked off, not wanting to see her emotions, as tears were already welled in her eyes. She shouted from a distance. "Your story doesn't have to end like this, though, Prince. It really and truly does not have to end like this!"

I kept it moving, before zooming off in my Camaro. Making my way down Page Boulevard, I was having a déjà vu moment. I thought about the day Nadine was killed and the mission I was on to murder those who were responsible.

*I knew exactly where her killers, Cedric and his crew, hung out, but before I even got to my destination, I spotted the burgundy Regal, which they drove while shooting up my car, parked in front of an auto body shop on the north side. Three of the niggas, including the one who had robbed me, stood outside laughing with the owner of the shop. They appeared to be having a funky good time, not even caring that Nadine's mother was somewhere grieving for her child. Yeah, it could have been my mother that time around, but it was painful to see Nadine's mother carry on at the hospital the way she did. I kept my eyes on Ced and his crew that day, and when they walked across the street to a lounge, I parked my car and changed my blood-soiled shirt with a clean one I'd had on the back seat. I waited for fifteen minutes, contemplating my next move. I thought about my son living without a mother and father. Damn, I didn't want him being raised by Mama, and I knew that Nadine's mother was so upset with me that she'd probably want no part of him. Without me, he was guaranteed a fucked-up life.*

*Even with me, he was too. Maybe what I did that day wasn't the right thing to do, but when I looked at all of the dried blood splattered on my front seat, maybe it was necessary. As I was in thought, I remembered my cell phone ringing. It was my sister, Patrice. I started not to answer my phone, but instead I did.*

*"Prince," she repeated, barely hearing my voice when I answered.*

*"What?"*

*"Why are you sounding like that?"*

*"Because I . . . I just wanna kill somebody right now, that's why."*

*"Who are you fighting with now? I hope you and your mother aren't at it again."*

*I wiped my tears, skeptical about telling her what had happened. "Nadine's dead. She got shot and I know the niggas who did it."*

*She hesitated to speak, but then spoke up. "I'm sorry to hear about Nadine, but you have to step back and let the police handle that. Pleeeease."*

*She sounded just like Poetry, but why wasn't I listening?*

*"They ain't gon' handle shit and you know it. I'm gon' handle it, fasho."*

*"Go to the police now, Prince. This thing is much bigger than you. And remember, it's up to you to change course. Millionaires are leaders, and followers like our father wind up dead or in jail. Don't be like Derrick, please. That's not what you want, is it? God said the vengeance is His—"*

*"Yeah, yeah, yeah . . . I got that. But today it may have to be mine."*

*I hung up on Patrice, only because I was being interrupted by numerous calls from Mama's phone.*

*"What?" I answered.*

*"Where are you?" she shouted.*

*"Out."*

*"Out where, Prince? Don't be out there doin' nothin' stupid and you need to get back here so you can see about your son. All this bullshit . . ." I heard Raylo saying something in the background, then he took the phone.*

*"He ain't tryin' to hear yo' gotdamn mouth! Move back and silence yourself, woman. Young blood," he said. "Handle yo' business. That's what real niggas do, and make sure that wherever you are, you don't be the one leavin' in no body bag. Pump two for me and I expect to see you at your mama's house within the hour, pickin' up yo' son and goin' on with yo' life. Stay up."*

*Raylo hung up and I closed my eyes, listening to the many voices in my head. Sometimes decisions like this didn't come easy. People thought they did, but I didn't grow up saying that I wanted to be a murderer.*

But at that point, I felt like I did now . . . What choice did I have?

*I heard Patrice pleading with me in her soft-spoken voice: step back and let the police handle it. "Pleeease. Don't be like Derrick." Then, Mama's voice got at me: "You need to get back here so you can see about your son. Raylo: "Handle yo' business. That's what real niggas do. Don't leave in no body bag and get those niggas!" He sounded like the devil, making his noise, and I hated like hell to let the devil have his way. Then, there was another voice. It shouted so loud that my eyes popped open. "Vengeance is mine!" the powerful voice said. "All mine!"*

Yet again, I was in a similar situation. Raylo was about to see what real niggas do. For me, he had been the devil all along, making this time much easier than the first. There was no hesitation on my part, and even though that same voice was trying to get in my head about vengeance, I wasn't trying to hear it.

The light turned yellow and I slowed down so I wouldn't run it. Normally, I would have, but since I saw a police officer's car ahead, I changed my mind. I yawned, and when I reached up to straighten my rearview mirror, I saw headlights coming fast from behind. It didn't look like the car was going to stop, and before I could swerve my car over to the side, the other car slammed into the back of me. I wasn't wearing a seat belt, so my body flew forward and my head slammed against the windshield. After being thrown around, I flopped back in my seat and my eyes were too heavy to stay open. Minutes later, I saw darkness.


As I slowly cracked my eyes, I didn't know what day or time it was. I could tell I was in the hospital just from the smell, the nurse standing in front of me, and the white walls. A TV was hanging from above and I was covered in white sheets. My whole body ached all over and I could feel a patch on the left side of my face. I lifted my hand to touch it, but the pressure that I put on it made it so sore.

The nurse leaned over me. "How are you feeling?" she asked.

I tried to open my mouth, but was barely able to mumble. "Okay, I guess. How . . . how long have I been in here and what happened?"

"You were in a serious car accident. You've been in here for almost two weeks and today is your birthday. Do you know your name?"

"Prin . . . Jamal Prince Perkins."

"How old are you?"

"Twenty-one."

"Mother's name?"

"Shante Perkins."

"Good," the nurse said, patting my arm. "What a blessing that you're alive and seem to be doin' well. Let me go get the doctor so you can talk to him."

The nurse left the room, and I struggled to sit up straight. Somehow I managed, and when I looked over by the window, I saw several Happy Birthday cards. I tried to remember what I was doing before the accident, then it came to me. I was on my way to take care of Raylo. I remembered the headlights approaching me from behind, and after that, I couldn't remember anything else.

The doctor came into the room, smiling and standing next to me with a chart. "You're feeling okay?" he asked.

I nodded. "Still in some pain, and my body feels stiff."

"Once you get up and start walking around, you'll be okay. You had a concussion, and were in a coma for a while. You got banged up pretty good, but the bruises and swelling should go down over time. I'll give you something for the pain, then we'll get you something to eat. How does that sound?"

I nodded again. The doctor talked to me about running several more tests to make sure everything checked out with me, then he walked out. Shortly after, the nurse returned with pain pills and a tray of dinner.

"Anything in particular that you want to watch on TV?"

"No, not really. Thanks, though."

The nurse made sure I was comfortable by sitting me up and fluffing my pillows. She put the tray right in front of me and poured my apple juice into a cup. I don't think I ever remembered a white woman being as nice to me as this one truly was.

"If you need anything else, use this to buzz me," she said, showing me the device to use. She left the room and I started to slowly eat the mashed potatoes and creamy corn. After two bites, I looked up and saw Poetry come into the room. Her arm was in a sling and a long scratch was on the top of her forehead. She was all smiles and walked right up to me.

"How'd you know I was here?" I asked, squinting from the pain on my face. "And what happened to you?"

She put her hand on her hip. "Duh, don't you know? You're here because of me. If you thought I was going to let you go do something so stupid, you were sadly mistaken."

I dropped my fork on the plate. "Did you . . . Was that you in that car behind me?"

She smiled. "Yep, that would be me. I'm sorry for tearing your car up like that, but my insurance will pay for it, or buy you another one because that one may be totaled. My car pretty banged up too, and next time, please, please put on your seatbelt. I can't believe you wasn't wearing your seat belt."

I was almost too stunned to talk. "Ma, yo' ass is crazy! You could have killed both of us going that fast. Why put your life at risk like that?"

She bent over the bed and came closer to me. "Because I didn't want you to get hurt by nobody but me. I hurt myself in the process, and when the policeman saw what I'd done, he charged me with reckless driving and arrested me. I have a scheduled court date, and I hope the fine or punishment ain't going to be too steep." She shrugged and chuckled. "Besides, I owed you that for driving your motorcycle fast that day, and if I am crazy, I'm only crazy about you. I had to stop you, Prince, and I didn't see no other way to do it."

I was still in shock by what Poetry had done, and I hoped that she didn't find herself in a heap of trouble because of me. Still, my words were clipped tight and I didn't know what to say about this chick. I had definitely met my match and that was without a doubt.

"Sooo, what you got planned once you get out of here?" she asked. "It can't be about no trigger-happy shit, and just so you know, Mr. Street Soldier, Raylo was arrested last week for the murder of your mother. His fingerprints were all over the knife they found, and according to some very important people I know, I heard he confessed to your mama's murder. So, it's bye-bye little birdie for him. I'm sure you never have to worry about him again, and time to wash your hands of the whole situation." She paused, then put her hand on her hips. "Also, that dude G? Can you believe that somebody cut up that fool's body and threw him in a dumpster? If you wasn't in this bed all messed up, I sure would have thought it was you who had done it. Then again, I can't ever see you cutting nobody up."

"Nah, I wouldn't do nothin' like that. Must have been somebody hatin' on him real bad."

"I know, right. That mess was all over the news and, as usual, they have no suspects and no motive. See, sometimes you gotta step aside and let the Man upstairs handle His business, 'cause when we try to do it, we fuck up." Poetry looked up. "Oops, excuse me, Lord, my bad. Anyway, with Raylo and G out of the way, I was hoping that you would hook back up with your girlfriend and start doing the right thing. I don't need no Clint Eastwood, and all I need is a man to love, respect, and take care of me. Can you handle that for me, or is that asking for too much?"

I closed my eyes, feeling so much relief inside. To know that Raylo confessed made me angry, but I felt as if so many heavy burdens had been lifted off me. To know that he was behind bars, that was somewhat of a good thing. I damn sure wanted to take care of him myself, but it was too late for that kind of thinking. I didn't expect for all of my troubles to go away, but this was a good start. I could have jumped out of bed and kissed Poetry all over. But the way my body was feeling, I couldn't get too excited.

Poetry folded her arms and tapped her foot on the floor. "Come on now, birthday boy, say something? Are you down with me, mister, or what?"

I smiled and let off a soft snicker, mumbling, "Yeah, I'm down."

She moved closer to me and put her hand behind her ear. "I can't hear you. You gon' have to speak louder than that!"

"Yes, I'm down," I said a little louder, but loud enough where it made my head throb.

"No Clint Eastwood, Scarface, no Billy the Kid . . . none of that, right?"

I couldn't help but laugh. "No. Just Jamal Prince Perkins. Your Street Soldier who is no longer at war."

"Yaaay," Poetry said, playfully jumping around. "Prince got a girlfriend, Prince got a girlfriend, Prince got a girlfriend. . . ."

I sure did have a girlfriend. One I intended to someday raise my son with, who I counted on to keep me out of trouble, and one I would one day marry and love forever. She was the real soldier and I couldn't help but to be happy about Miss Poetry Wright coming into my life. Maybe all that stuff about guardian angels really was true, 'cause somebody around was damn sure looking out for me.

# Notes

# Notes

# Notes

ORDER FORM
URBAN BOOKS, LLC
78 E. Industry Ct
Deer Park, NY 11729

Name:(please print):_____

Address:        _____

City/State:     _____

Zip:            _____

| QTY | TITLES | PRICE |
|-----|--------|-------|
|     |        |       |
|     |        |       |
|     |        |       |
|     |        |       |
|     |        |       |
|     |        |       |
|     |        |       |
|     |        |       |
|     |        |       |
|     |        |       |
|     |        |       |
|     |        |       |

Shipping and handling-add $3.50 for 1st book, then $1.75 for each additional book.

Please send a check payable to:

**Urban Books, LLC**

Please allow 4-6 weeks for delivery

## ORDER FORM
## URBAN BOOKS, LLC
78 E. Industry Ct
Deer Park, NY 11729

Name: (please print):_____

Address:    _____

City/State:  _____

Zip:       _____

| QTY | TITLES | PRICE |
|---|---|---|
|  | 16 On The Block | $14.95 |
|  | A Girl From Flint | $14.95 |
|  | A Pimp's Life | $14.95 |
|  | Baltimore Chronicles | $14.95 |
|  | Baltimore Chronicles 2 | $14.95 |
|  | Betrayal | $14.95 |
|  | Black Diamond | $14.95 |
|  | Black Diamond 2 | $14.95 |
|  | Black Friday | $14.95 |
|  | Both Sides Of The Fence | $14.95 |
|  | Both Sides Of The Fence 2 | $14.95 |
|  | California Connection | $14.95 |

Shipping and handling-add $3.50 for 1st book, then $1.75 for each additional book.
Please send a check payable to:
**Urban Books, LLC**
Please allow 4-6 weeks for delivery

## ORDER FORM
## URBAN BOOKS, LLC
78 E. Industry Ct
Deer Park, NY 11729

Name: (please print):_____

Address:        _____

City/State:     _____

Zip:            _____

| QTY | TITLES | PRICE |
|---|---|---|
|  | California Connection 2 | $14.95 |
|  | Cheesecake And Teardrops | $14.95 |
|  | Congratulations | $14.95 |
|  | Crazy In Love | $14.95 |
|  | Cyber Case | $14.95 |
|  | Denim Diaries | $14.95 |
|  | Diary Of A Mad First Lady | $14.95 |
|  | Diary Of A Stalker | $14.95 |
|  | Diary Of A Street Diva | $14.95 |
|  | Diary Of A Young Girl | $14.95 |
|  | Dirty Money | $14.95 |
|  | Dirty To The Grave | $14.95 |

Shipping and handling-add $3.50 for 1st book, then $1.75 for each additional book.

Please send a check payable to:

**Urban Books, LLC**

Please allow 4-6 weeks for delivery

ORDER FORM
URBAN BOOKS, LLC
78 E. Industry Ct
Deer Park, NY 11729

Name:(please print):_____

Address:        _____

City/State:     _____

Zip:            _____

| QTY | TITLES | PRICE |
|-----|--------|-------|
|  | Gunz And Roses | $14.95 |
|  | Happily Ever Now | $14.95 |
|  | Hell Has No Fury | $14.95 |
|  | Hush | $14.95 |
|  | If It Isn't love | $14.95 |
|  | Kiss Kiss Bang Bang | $14.95 |
|  | Last Breath | $14.95 |
|  | Little Black Girl Lost | $14.95 |
|  | Little Black Girl Lost 2 | $14.95 |
|  | Little Black Girl Lost 3 | $14.95 |
|  | Little Black Girl Lost 4 | $14.95 |
|  | Little Black Girl Lost 5 | $14.95 |

Shipping and handling-add $3.50 for 1st book, then $1.75 for each additional book.
Please send a check payable to:
**Urban Books, LLC**
Please allow 4-6 weeks for delivery

## ORDER FORM
## URBAN BOOKS, LLC
78 E. Industry Ct
Deer Park, NY 11729

Name: (please print): _____

Address: _____

City/State: _____

Zip: _____

| QTY | TITLES | PRICE |
|---|---|---|
| | Loving Dasia | $14.95 |
| | Material Girl | $14.95 |
| | Moth To A Flame | $14.95 |
| | Mr. High Maintenance | $14.95 |
| | My Little Secret | $14.95 |
| | Naughty | $14.95 |
| | Naughty 2 | $14.95 |
| | Naughty 3 | $14.95 |
| | Queen Bee | $14.95 |
| | Say It Ain't So | $14.95 |
| | Snapped | $14.95 |
| | Snow White | $14.95 |

Shipping and handling-add $3.50 for 1st book, then $1.75 for each additional book.
Please send a check payable to:
**Urban Books, LLC**
Please allow 4-6 weeks for delivery

## ORDER FORM
## URBAN BOOKS, LLC
## 78 E. Industry Ct
## Deer Park, NY 11729

Name: (please print): _____

Address: _____

City/State: _____

Zip: _____

| QTY | TITLES | PRICE |
|---|---|---|
| | Spoil Rotten | $14.95 |
| | Supreme Clientele | $14.95 |
| | The Cartel | $14.95 |
| | The Cartel 2 | $14.95 |
| | The Cartel 3 | $14.95 |
| | The Dopefiend | $14.95 |
| | The Dopeman Wife | $14.95 |
| | The Prada Plan | $14.95 |
| | The Prada Plan 2 | $14.95 |
| | Where There Is Smoke | $14.95 |
| | Where There Is Smoke 2 | $14.95 |
| | | |

Shipping and handling-add $3.50 for 1st book, then $1.75 for each additional book.

Please send a check payable to:

**Urban Books, LLC**

Please allow 4-6 weeks for delivery

## ORDER FORM
## URBAN BOOKS, LLC
### 78 E. Industry Ct
### Deer Park, NY 11729

Name:(please print):_____

Address:     _____

City/State:   _____

Zip:         _____

| QTY | TITLES | PRICE |
|-----|--------|-------|
|     |        |       |
|     |        |       |
|     |        |       |
|     |        |       |
|     |        |       |
|     |        |       |
|     |        |       |
|     |        |       |
|     |        |       |
|     |        |       |
|     |        |       |
|     |        |       |

Shipping and handling-add \$3.50 for 1$^{st}$ book, then \$1.75 for each additional book.

Please send a check payable to:

**Urban Books, LLC**

Please allow 4-6 weeks for delivery

ORDER FORM
URBAN BOOKS, LLC
78 E. Industry Ct
Deer Park, NY 11729

Name: (please print):_____

Address:      _____

City/State:   _____

Zip:          _____

| QTY | TITLES | PRICE |
|-----|--------|-------|
|     |        |       |
|     |        |       |
|     |        |       |
|     |        |       |
|     |        |       |
|     |        |       |
|     |        |       |
|     |        |       |
|     |        |       |
|     |        |       |
|     |        |       |
|     |        |       |

Shipping and handling-add $3.50 for 1st book, then $1.75 for each additional book.

Please send a check payable to:

**Urban Books, LLC**

Please allow 4-6 weeks for delivery